A Fantasy of Dr Ox

A Fantasy of Dr Ox

Jules Verne

Translated by Andrew Brown

ET REMOTISSIMA PROPE

100 PAGES

100 PAGES

Published by Hesperus Press Limited

4 Rickett Street, London sw6 1ru

www.hesperuspress.com

First published in French as *Une fantaisie du docteur Ox* in 1872

This translation first published by Hesperus Press Limited, 2003

Introduction and English language translation © Andrew Brown, 2003

Foreword © Gilbert Adair, 2003

Designed and typeset by Fraser Muggeridge

Printed in the United Arab Emirates by Oriental Press

ISBN: 1-84391-067-5

CONTENTS

FOREWORD

The genre of science fiction has traditionally been defended by its champions as the literary form best fitted to address, in the mode of the thinly camouflaged parable, a host of contentious issues endemic to contemporary society – most notably the fate of individual free will in a world fuelled, even ruled, by information technology. As someone who finds virtually all of science fiction indigestible, and who tends to be as alienated by its relentlessly neologistic terminology, by words like 'bionic', 'space-warp' and 'cyberborg', as others are by the instructions in a DVD manual, I am prepared to accept such a defence on faith – provided it is never tested on me. At the same time, I have always been an unconditional admirer of Jules Verne, sci-fi's supreme pioneer, and it was while pondering this apparent contradiction that I arrived at an alternative, whimsical, but also, for anyone who shares my distaste, more user-friendly approach to the genre. What I would propose is that a work of science fiction may be judged of interest and significance *only* if it remains readable after the passing of the date in which its action is set (as with Orwell's *Nineteen Eighty-four*, to take the most obvious example); hence, by extension, that all 'futuristic' novels are in fact best read *only* after years, ideally centuries, have elapsed since their original publication.

Viewed from this angle, Verne's science fiction, like that of his main rival, H.G. Wells, is only now ripe for reading. It has, for us, layers of meaning it could not have had for its author's own nineteenth-century contemporaries. For it is set, *as only we are capable of understanding*, neither in the future nor in the past but in a unique tense that has become, with the passage of time, a weird amalgam of both – what might be defined as the conditional.

A case in point is a little-known, only recently published novel of his, *Paris in the 20th Century*. Verne wrote it in 1863 (or so it is speculated – its history is a vexed one) just prior to the successful publication of his official Opus 1, *Five Weeks in a Balloon*. It was instantly rejected by his publisher-to-be, Hetzel, as artless and crude. It vanished, long thought to have been lost for ever, until its reapparition in the late 1990s. And it is set in the Paris of 1960.

That circuitous train of circumstances constitutes precisely, for me, the source of its fascination. If I had chanced to encounter the novel in 1863, I should certainly have agreed with Hetzel; reading it nearly a century and a half later, however, I found it utterly absorbing. Simply to see the date '1960' on the printed page, *as written by Jules Verne*, provoked a frisson in itself, as if there were something authentically supernatural about the very existence of such a book. By contrast, mere mention of, let's say, a date such as '3075' in current science fiction is enough to have me nodding off.

As for *A Fantasy of Dr Ox*, it may seem, in this respect as in others, untypical of Verne's teeming imagination; and, possibly for that reason, it has remained nearly as little known as *Paris in the 20th Century* (even if it boasts the rare distinction of having been twice adapted for the operatic – or, rather, 'operettic' – stage, once by Offenbach and once again by the British composer Gavin Bryars). In the first place, it is a novella, not a full-length novel. In the second, it is a frankly comic work; and although humour has seldom been absent from Verne's novels (apart from all those eccentrically droll professors who populate his sci-fi romances, think of the Don Quixote-Sancho Panza double act of Phileas Fogg and his manservant Passepartout in *Around the World in Eighty Days*), he wrote next to nothing else designed, as *A Fantasy of Dr Ox* is, to make the reader laugh out loud (which, incidentally, it does more than once). And, in the third, the strict science-fictional element, although by no means peripheral (it is, on the contrary, absolutely crucial) to the plotline, was for once, in the context of the novella's publication year, 1874, technically more or less doable and thus not all that prophetic.

What is the plotline? Briefly: the mysterious Ox and his assistant Ygène (i.e. ox+ygène), having somehow inveigled the burgomaster of an outlandishly dozy Flemish hamlet, Quiquendone, into commissioning them to install gas street lighting throughout the town, elect rather, in the cause of (extremely dubious) scientific experimentation, to pump out pure oxygen. Suddenly, the normally placid Quiquendonians find themselves raising their voices and fists at one another for the very first time in living memory; fights break out in public places; and, in one outrageous set piece, the staging of a single act of Meyerbeer's ponderous grand opera *Les Huguenots* takes – instead of the six hours (repeat: *six hours*) it might be expected to do if conducted and sung at the stupefyingly slow tempi preferred by the locals – just eighteen minutes.

In short, these chronically, and, we are led to believe, congenitally bovine locals are gradually driven to the verge of madness by this quotidian 'fix', this personality-altering 'high', of which they are the unwitting recipients. In the 1870s, when *A Fantasy of Dr Ox* was first published, that was already a wonderful comic conceit. But what makes the novella so much richer and subtler a reading experience today is that only we are aware that, even in this squib, Verne's foresight was amazing, since what he portrayed, in his depiction of a community fallen victim to collective stress, with each member of that community surrendering to the selfishly solipsistic frenzy of the moment, was a combination of all the so-called 'rages' which have proved to be the bane of urban life in the twenty-first century – road rage, air rage, restaurant rage, etc. What he anticipated, then, a hundred and fifty years before the event, was 'life rage'.

– Gilbert Adair, 2003

INTRODUCTION

The great conductor Otto Klemperer is famous, or infamous, for the increasing slowness of tempo of his performances of the classics of Western music. Peter Heyworth once asked him, when he was a Grand Old Man of conducting, how he could tell what the right speed for a piece of music was. 'One feels it,' replied Klemperer. 'I mean, it was characteristic of Mahler's conducting that one felt that the tempo could not be otherwise.' When Heyworth went on to ask whether he thought his own tempi had become slower, Klemperer demurred, and became a little defensive when Heyworth started quoting particular examples from his recordings that did indeed suggest that he had slowed down over the years. Accounts of these recordings frequently contrast their slowness with the quicker versions of other conductors – Toscanini, for instance, whom Klemperer on occasion found 'much too fast' and who often seemed the opposite of Klemperer, speeding up to a mad dash as he got older. And there are even more notorious cases of slow conductors, such as Reginald Goodall, whose Wagner performances are distinguished by, to put it politely, an extreme broadness of tempo. In some of the repertoire conducted by Klemperer, the question of 'historically informed performance' (agreeably abbreviated to HIP) has come to the fore in the last twenty years: the listener can now contrast the version of Bach's Mass in B Minor conducted by the 'hare-like Franz Brueggen' with that of the 'tortoise-like old man' Klemperer, though the question as to whose speeds are more 'authentic' (i.e. closer to those imagined by Bach) still provokes lively scholarly debate.

What is the right speed for a piece of music? Perhaps there is no 'right' speed; perhaps no one speed is right all the time.

And the different participants (performers and listeners) in music may experience the same piece at different tempi. (Sir Thomas Beecham to the dancers at the beginning of a ballet rehearsal: 'What shall it be today? Too fast or too slow?')

What is the right speed at which to live one's life? Should you be a tortoise or a hare? (It's true that, in the fable, the tortoise wins the race, but is it worth it?) Verne's *A Fantasy of Dr Ox* is a short, slight piece, economical in style, light-hearted in manner, told with brio and at a brisk allegro vivace, yet, as so often with Verne, the apparent superficiality of manner touches on themes whose slow echoes continue to resonate in the mind long after one has read the story. The inhabitants of the Flemish city of Quiquendone lead lives of extraordinary slowness and tranquillity. Their heartbeats rarely rise above fifty to the minute. Their taste in music runs to performances of lavish leisureliness. Klemperer at his most tortoise-like would have struck them as dashing through the music in indecent haste, as if anxious that he might miss, as it were, closing time at the musicians' bar. And they would have run Toscanini out of town (or presumably accompanied him gravely to the Oudenaarde Gate and put him on a slow train to Brussels).

All this changes with the arrival of the scientist Dr Ox and his assistant Ygène. Despite the reference to bovine disease at one moment in the text, the reader soon realises that the story is not about the hygiene of oxen (of course, of course – but Verne teases the reader: has he or she been quicker on the uptake than the initially stolid Quiquendonians? Understanding the story too quickly might spoil the rhythm of suspense and disclosure that is part of the charm of the narrative – its comic timing). One of the effects of Ox's experiment is to speed up the tempo of the locals to the point where they can shake off their sluggishness (Flemings are phlegmatic) and become more choleric (Flanders is a place of flame). One of the first indices of this change is indeed in the pace at which they like their music – and, here, the comic-opera potentials of the story immediately become apparent. The first of the two musical adaptations – by Offenbach – Verne supposedly didn't much care for; perhaps he would have preferred the second, more recent one by Gavin Bryars (*Dr Ox's Experiment*), with its libretto by Blake Morrison, first produced by Atom Egoyan.

Ox is to some extent one of Verne's mad scientists: an outsider figure who comes to town, uses its inhabitants as his guinea pigs, creates havoc, and then vanishes with a bang that is more Mephistophelean than Faustian. His assistant Ygène is a little hesitant about the experiment (closer in temperament to the Quiquendonians, whose whole life is one long hesi-tation): he registers a doubt about the hasty amorality of his scientific and modernising master. And yet it is not certain that the story is so very 'scientific', despite having at times been acclaimed as an early (and still rare) example of comic science fiction (the latter tending, especially from Mary Shelley's *Frankenstein* onwards, to be doom-laden and apocalyptic). It is true that, as Blake Morrison has pointed out, Verne might have been interested in the experiments of Paul Bert, a French physiologist who exposed animals to a treatment similar to that inflicted on the Quiquendonians by Dr Ox. It is also true that Verne's story was written in 1871, at a time when naturalism was increasingly setting the agenda for French fiction. Zola's preface to the second edition of his *Thérèse Raquin* (1868) disavows any moral intent, and at the same time any emotional empathy with (or disgust at) his sexually enthralled protagonists Thérèse and her lover Laurent. They are simply the products of the 'inexorable laws' of their physical natures, and any remorse they feel for killing off Thérèse's husband Camille is itself a mere 'organic disorder'. Circumstance and environment ('atmosphere', one might say, to bring out the parallel with Quiquendone) determine the characters without their being able to do anything about it. Hippolyte Taine stated that 'vice and virtue are products like vitriol and sugar', a view that strongly influenced Zola. But Zola was not a scientist, or at least his work is not exhausted by the truth content or otherwise of the scientific themes it touches on. Verne, too, may or may not believe that behaviour we normally consider to be 'good' or 'bad' is explicable by purely material and physiological causes. But that is not the point. He is not out to prove anything: the Hetzel version of his story included a few words distancing himself from his eponymous hero's theory: 'we have every right not to accept it, *and for our part we reject it from every point of view*, despite his whimsical experiment [etc.]'. Whereas the British musical adaptation gives the title *Dr Ox's Experiment*, the story's original title places the emphasis on the 'fantasy' (or whim, or act of imagination): it is not a real experiment, but a thought experiment, and perhaps not even that – a fable, or, quite simply, a short story, to be enjoyed for the many trains of thought it starts without letting any of them reach a destination. Before we realise what is really causing the speed-ups and slow-downs of the Quiquendonians, it is entertaining to think of them as merely suffering from an acute form of bipolar affective disorder, swinging from mania to depression within minutes, like a man who leaves his girlfriend full of intense and starry-eyed love, only to decide, by the time he reaches home, that he never wants to see her again, and phones her up to tell her so. Dr Ox's experiment makes the Quiquendonians live more intensely – a blessing or a curse? They will die younger, but live 'more'; instead of vegetating, they will 'burn'. Instead of living in peace and brotherly love – and inventing the cuckoo clock (and, admittedly, democracy), like the Swiss according to Harry Lime in *The Third Man* – they will have internecine wars and manic productivity and maybe the Borgias, like Renaissance Italians. (One of the blessings, or, if you prefer, curses of Dr Ox's experiment is that the Quiquendonians start to get passionate about politics.) The idea of a small town in Flanders suddenly deciding to go to war with an equally small town over a trivial centuries-old trespass by a cow is partly Swiftian (Lilliput versus Brobdingnag: not 'go to work on an egg', but 'go to war over an egg') and partly reminiscent of an Ealing Comedy (*Passport to Pimlico*, perhaps, in which martial ardour is likewise inflamed by a long-forgotten deed), or Chesterton's *The Napoleon of Notting Hill*. Or, indeed, of such mock-epics as the skit on Homer known as the *Batrachomyomachia*, or *Battle of Frogs and Mice*. But age-old skirmishes over a patch of land, and apparently trivial slights, have always had consequences that transcend the mock-epic: small causes lead to an accelerando and crescendo of effect. Award the prize to the 'wrong' goddess and Troy goes up in flames. And in any case, Flanders, home of the still life, the late-medieval form of the *vita contemplativa* known as the *devotio moderna*, and clearly characterised by Verne as a place of bovine content-ment, was also always the cockpit of Europe. Look on any map and you will see how close Quiquendone is to Ypres and Mons: forty years after Verne's story was written, the fields of Flanders were inflamed by a conflict that combined, with unprecedented savagery, the speed and violence of modern technology and the passion of territorial disputes on the one hand, and the monumental slowness of trench warfare on the other, with the gentle landscapes of Memling being torn apart by rampaging hordes from Bosch or the 'Dulle Griet' of Brueghel. One particular form of the new technology might have attracted the interest of Verne's protagonist: the use of chemical weapons. *Oh What a Lovely War*; or, as Dr Ox might have put it, *what a gas*.

– *Andrew Brown, 2003*

Note on the Text:
The edition used is that included in *Contes et nouvelles de Jules Verne* (Rennes: Éditions Ouest-France, 2000).

A Fantasy of Dr Ox

Why it is pointless looking for the small town of Quiquendone, even on the best maps

If you take a map of Flanders, old or new, and start looking for the small town of Quiquendone, it is quite probable you won't find it. So is Quiquendone a vanished town? No. A town of the future? Again, no. It exists in spite of the geographers, and has done so for between eight and nine hundred years. Indeed, it has a population of 2,393 souls, if you reckon one soul for each inhabitant. It is situated thirteen and a half kilometres north-west of Oudenaarde and fifteen and a quarter kilometres south-east of Bruges, in the middle of Flanders. The Vaar, a small tributary of the Scheldt, flows beneath its three bridges that are still covered by an old medieval roof, as at Tournay. One of the sights is an old castle, the first stone of which was laid in 1197 by Count Baldwin, the future Emperor of Constantinople, and a town hall with gothic half-windows, crowned by a row of battlements and dominated by a turreted belfry, rising 357 feet above the ground. Every hour you can hear the peal of five octaves, a veritable aerial piano, whose renown surpasses that of the famous peal at Bruges. Strangers – if any have ever come to Quiquendone – never leave this curious town without having visited its hall of stadtholders, decorated with the full-length portrait of William of Nassau by Brandon, and the rood screen of the church of Saint-Magloire, that masterpiece of sixteenth-century architecture; or the forged-iron well dug into the middle of the great Place Saint-Ernuph, the admirable ornamentation on which is the work of the painter and ironsmith Quentin Metsys; or the tomb provisionally erected for Mary of Burgundy, daughter of

Charles the Bold, who now rests in the church of Notre-Dame in Bruges, etc. Quiquendone's main industry is the large-scale manufacture of whipped cream and barley-sugar. It has been administered for several centuries by the van Tricasse family, passing down from father to son. And yet Quiquendone doesn't appear on the map of Flanders! Have the geographers forgotten it? Is it a deliberate omission? That's what I can't tell you: but Quiquendone really *does* exist, with its narrow streets, its fortified enclosure, its Spanish houses, its covered market and its burgomaster – the proof being that it was recently the scene of phenomena as surprising, extraordinary, and improbable as they are true, as will be faithfully related in this story.

Of course, there's nothing to be said or thought against the Flemish inhabitants of western Flanders. They're decent people, sensible, a bit tight-fisted, sociable, even-tempered, hospitable, perhaps a bit slow in speech and not very quick on the uptake, but that doesn't explain why one of the most interesting towns on their territory still has to make it into modern cartography.

This omission is certainly regrettable. If only history, or, if not history, then the chronicles, or, if not the chronicles, at least local tradition made some mention of Quiquendone! But they don't; neither atlases nor guides nor tourist routes refer to it. M. Joanne himself, always conscientious at ferreting out little towns, doesn't have a word to say about it.[1] It's easy to imagine how much harm this silence does to the town's commerce and industry. But let us hasten to add that Quiquendone has neither industry nor commerce, and that it manages perfectly well without them. Its barley-sugar and its whipped cream are consumed by the inhabitants and not exported. In short, the Quiquendonians don't need anyone.

Their desires are limited, their way of life modest; they are calm, moderate, cold, phlegmatic, in a word, 'Flemish', of the kind you still encounter sometimes between the River Scheldt and the North Sea.

*In which Burgomaster van Tricasse and Councillor
Niklausse discuss the affairs of the town*

'Do you think so?' asked the burgomaster.

'I do think so,' replied the councillor, after a few minutes' silence.

'We mustn't act without due consideration,' the burgomaster continued.

'We have been talking about this highly serious matter for ten years,' replied Councillor Niklausse, 'and I must confess, my worthy van Tricasse, that I still cannot bring myself to take a decision.'

'I can understand your hesitation,' continued the burgomaster, after spending a good quarter of an hour mulling it over, 'I can understand your hesitation and I share it. The sensible thing will be not to come to any decision before we've examined the question in more detail.'

'It's certain that this post of civil commissioner is useless in a town as peaceful as Quiquendone.'

'Our predecessor,' replied van Tricasse gravely, 'our predecessor never said, would never have dared to say, that anything is certain. Every affirmation is subject to disagreeable second thoughts.'

The councillor nodded in agreement, then he remained silent for about half an hour. After this lapse of time, during which the councillor and the burgomaster didn't move so much as a finger, Niklausse asked van Tricasse if his predecessor – some twenty years previously – hadn't entertained, as he had, the idea of suppressing this post of civil commissioner which, every year, cost the town of

Quiquendone a sum of 1,375 francs and several centimes.

'He had indeed,' replied the burgomaster, who with majestic slowness brought his hand up to his limpid brow, 'he had indeed; but the worthy man died before daring to take a decision on this or any other administrative measure. He was a sensible fellow. Why shouldn't I follow his example?'

Councillor Niklausse would have been incapable of imagining any reason for contradicting the burgomaster's opinion.

'The man who dies without ever having taken a decision all his life long,' added van Tricasse gravely, 'has come close to achieving perfection in this world!'

Upon these words, the burgomaster pressed, with the tip of his little finger, a bell which emitted a faint sound, less a sound than a sigh. Almost immediately, light footsteps were heard padding softly along the tiles of the landing. A mouse would have made less noise trotting across a thick velvet-pile carpet. The door of the room opened, turning on its well-oiled hinges. A young blond girl, with long plaits, appeared. She was Suzel van Tricasse, the burgomaster's only daughter. Without a word, she handed over to her father, together with his pipe filled to the brim, a little copper charcoal pan, and immediately disappeared, without her exit producing any more sound than her entrance.

The honourable burgomaster lit the enormous bowl of his smoking instrument, and was soon hidden in a cloud of bluish smoke, leaving Councillor Niklausse sunk deep in the most absorbing reflections.

The room in which these two eminent personages responsible for the administration of Quiquendone were talking was a parlour richly decorated with sculptures in dark wood. A tall fireplace, a hearth huge enough to burn an oak tree or roast an ox, occupied one entire side of the parlour, and faced a trellis window whose multicoloured stained-glass windows gently filtered the daylight. In an antique frame, over the fireplace, could be seen the portrait of some fellow or other, attributed to Memling; it was no doubt meant to represent an ancestor of the van Tricasse family, whose genealogy can be authentically traced back to the fourteenth century, a period in which the Flemish, and Guy of Dampierre, were involved in war against Emperor Rudolph of Hapsburg.

This parlour was part of the burgomaster's house, one of the most pleasant in Quiquendone. Built according to the Flemish taste and with all the eccentricity, whimsicality and picturesque fantasy that are essential to gothic architecture, it counted as one of the most curious of the town's monuments. A Carthusian monastery or an establishment for deaf mutes couldn't have been more silent than this dwelling. Noise simply did not exist in the place; people didn't walk through it, they glided along; they didn't speak, they murmured. And yet there was no shortage of women in the house which, apart from Burgomaster van Tricasse, also accommodated his wife, Mme Brigitte van Tricasse, his daughter Suzel van Tricasse, and his servant-woman Lotchè Janshéu. We must also mention the burgomaster's sister, Aunt Hermance, an old maid who still answered to the name Aunty Némance that her niece Suzel had given her when still a child. Anyway, in spite of all these elements of discord, noise and chatter, the burgo-master's house was as calm as the desert.

The burgomaster was a fifty-year-old man, neither fat nor thin, neither tall nor short, neither young nor old, neither florid nor pasty, neither happy nor sad, neither content nor bored, neither active nor passive, neither proud nor humble, neither good nor bad, neither generous nor mean, neither brave nor cowardly, neither too much nor too little – *ne quid nimis* – a man who showed moderation in all things. But from the unvarying slowness of his movements, his somewhat drooping lower jaw, his invariably raised upper eyelid, his forehead as smooth as a sheet of yellow copper and perfectly unwrinkled, and his inconspicuous muscles, a physiognomist would doubtless have recognised that Burgomaster van Tricasse was the very model of a phlegmatic character. Never – either in anger or in passion – had any sort of emotion speeded up the movements of this man's heart, or brought a flush to his face; never had his pupils contracted under the influence of a moment of anger, however fleeting. He was inevitably dressed in nice clothes, neither too wide nor too narrow, that he never managed to wear out. On his feet he wore big square-toed shoes with triple soles and silver buckles; their longevity was the despair of his shoemaker. On his head he wore a broad hat which dated from the period when Flanders was decisively separated from Holland, which meant that this venerable headpiece could be estimated to be forty years old.[2] But what do you expect? It is passions which wear out the body as much as the soul, and also wear out the clothes as much as the body; and our worthy burgomaster, apathetic, indolent, indifferent, could get passionate about nothing; he wore nothing out, certainly not himself, and for that very reason he was just the man needed to administer the city of Quiquendone and its tranquil inhabitants. The town, in fact, was no less calm than van Tricasse's house. Now it was in this peaceful dwelling that the burgomaster hoped to drink life to the lees, after seeing, of course, good Mme Brigitte van Tricasse, his wife, precede him to the grave, where she would certainly not find a repose any more profound than that she had been enjoying on earth for the last sixty years.

This merits an explanation.

The van Tricasse family could have been called, with justice, the *Jeannot*[3] family. Here's why:

Everyone knows that the knife of that typical character is just as famous as its proprietor and just as durable as he is, thanks to the endlessly repeated operation, which consists of replacing the handle when it is worn out and the blade when it has lost its edge. This was the absolutely identical operation that had been practised from time immemorial in the van Tricasse family – an operation to which nature had lent itself with a quite extraordinary indulgence. Ever since 1380, a newly widowed van Tricasse husband had invariably been seen to marry a van Tricasse wife younger than himself; when she in turn was widowed, she would remarry a van Tricasse man younger than herself; when he in turn was widowed… etc., without a break. Each of them died in turn with mechanical regularity. Now the worthy Mme Brigitte van Tricasse was on her second husband, and unless she failed in all her duties, she would inevitably precede her spouse into the other world, as he was ten years younger than she was, so as to make way for a new Mme van Tricasse. On this the honourable burgomaster was counting absolutely, so as not to break with the family traditions.

Such was this house, peaceful and silent, whose doors didn't creak, whose windows didn't shudder, whose polished floors didn't squeak, whose chimneys didn't rumble, whose weathervanes didn't squeal, whose furniture didn't groan, whose locks didn't jingle, and whose hosts moved about as silently as their shadows. The divine Harpocrates would certainly have chosen it for his Temple of Silence.[4]

3

*In which Commissioner Passauf makes an
entrance as noisy as it is unexpected*

When the interesting conversation between the councillor and the burgomaster that we reported earlier started, it was a quarter to three in the afternoon. It was at three forty-five that van Tricasse lit his vast pipe, which could contain a quart of tobacco, and it was only at five thirty-five that he came to the end of his smoke.

This whole time, the two conversation partners didn't exchange a single word.

At around six o'clock, the councillor, who always proceeded by preterition or aposiopesis,[5] resumed in these terms:

'And so our decision is?…'

'To decide nothing,' replied the burgomaster.

'I think that, at the end of the day, you're right, van Tricasse.'

'I think so too, Niklausse. We'll make a resolution regarding the civil commissioner when we are better informed… later on… We don't need to do anything for a whole month.'

'Or even a whole year,' replied Niklausse, unfolding his pocket handkerchief, which he proceeded to use with perfect discretion.

There was a new silence, which lasted for a good hour. Nothing disturbed this new halt in the conversation, not even the appearance of the household dog, honest Lento, who, no less phlegmatic than his master, came to take a polite turn round the parlour. Worthy dog! A model for all those of its species. Even if he'd been made of cardboard, with little wheels on his paws, he couldn't have made any less noise during his visit.

At around eight o'clock, after Lotchè had brought in the antique lamp with its frosted glass, the burgomaster said to the councillor:

'We don't have any urgent business to attend to, do we, Niklausse?'

'No, van Tricasse, not so far as I'm aware.'

'But didn't someone tell me,' the burgomaster asked, 'that the Oudenaarde Tower was in danger of imminent collapse?'

'Indeed it is,' replied the councillor, 'and to tell you the truth I wouldn't be at all surprised if one day or another it fell down and crushed some passer-by.'

'Oh!' continued the burgomaster, 'before any such misfortune happens, I do hope that we will have taken a decision regarding this tower.'

'I hope so too, van Tricasse.'

'There are more urgent questions to resolve.'

'Doubtless,' replied the councillor. 'The question of the leather market, for example.'

'Is it still on fire?' asked the burgomaster.

'Still on fire, as it has been for three weeks.'

'Didn't we decide in council to let it burn down?'

'Yes, van Tricasse, and at your suggestion.'

'Wasn't this the surest and simplest way to control the fire?'

'Indisputably.'

'Well, let's wait. Is that all?'

'That's all,' replied the councillor, scratching his forehead as if to reassure himself that he wasn't forgetting any important piece of business.

'Ah!' said the burgomaster, 'haven't you also heard about a leak that's threatening to flood the lower district of Saint-Jacques?'

'I have indeed,' replied the councillor. 'It is even rather annoying that this leak didn't happen above the leather market. It would naturally have doused the fire, and that would have spared us many of these discussions.'

'What do you expect, Niklausse?' replied the worthy burgomaster, 'there's nothing so illogical as accidents. There's no link between these ones, and we can't take advantage of the one to lessen the effects of the other, as we would wish.'

This acute observation coming from van Tricasse required some time to be fully appreciated by his interlocutor and friend.

'Ah yes, but,' continued Councillor Niklausse after a few moments, 'we haven't even mentioned our main business!'

'Which main business? Do you mean we have some main business?' asked the burgomaster.

'I should think so: the town lighting.'

'Ah, yes!' replied the burgomaster, 'Dr Ox's lighting?'

'Precisely. And?…'

'It's all happening, Niklausse,' replied the burgomaster. 'They are already proceeding to lay down the pipes, and the factory is completely finished.'

'Perhaps we went about this business in a bit too much of a hurry,' said the councillor, shaking his head.

'Perhaps,' replied the burgomaster, 'but our excuse is that Dr Ox is bearing all the expenses for his experiment. It won't cost us a penny.'

'True, that's our excuse. And then, we have to keep in step with the times. If the experiment succeeds, Quiquendone will be the first town in Flanders to be lit with that gas – oxy… What do they call it?'

'Oxyhydric gas.'

'If you say so – oxyhydric gas.'

Just then, the door opened, and Lotchè came in to announce to the burgomaster that his supper was ready.

Councillor Niklausse rose to take his leave of van Tricasse, who had worked up an appetite over so many decisions and so much business. Then it was arranged that they would summon, at a reasonably distant date, the council of notables, so as to decide whether they could come to a provisional decision on the truly decisive question of the Oudenaarde Tower.

Then the two worthy administrators went down to the door that opened onto the street, the one showing the other the way. When the councillor arrived on the last landing, he lit a little lamp to guide him through the dark streets of Quiquendone, still unilluminated by Dr Ox's lighting. The night was dark, as it was October, and the town was enveloped in a light, hazy mist.

Councillor Niklausse required a good quarter of an hour to make the preparations for his departure – having lit his lamp, he still had to put on his big clogs with their cowhide linings, and his thick sheepskin mittens; then he put up the fur collar of his overcoat, pulled his felt hat down over his eyes, took a firm hold of his heavy, crutch-handled umbrella, and made ready to step out.

Just as Lotchè, who was holding the light for her master, was about to pull back the bar on the door, there was a loud, unexpected noise outside.

Yes, however improbable it might seem, a noise, a real noise, such as the town had certainly not heard since the taking of the castle keep by the Spanish in 1513, a dreadful noise awoke the echoes that were sleeping so soundly in the old van Tricasse house. Someone was banging this door, so unravished until then by brutal hands! Someone was banging and hammering on it with a blunt instrument that could only be a gnarled stick wielded by a strong hand! The blows were interspersed with shouts and cries for help. They could distinctly hear these words:

'Monsieur van Tricasse! Burgomaster! Open up, quick, quick!'

The burgomaster and the councillor, absolutely dumbfounded, stared at each other without uttering a word. They simply couldn't imagine it. Even if someone had fired into the parlour a shot from the old culverin in the castle, that hadn't been used since 1285, the inhabitants of the van Tricasse house couldn't have been more 'flabbergasted'. We must be forgiven for using this word; it's rather colloquial, but in this case it's the *mot juste*.

Meanwhile, the blows, the cries, the pleas were becoming more insistent. Lotchè, regaining her calm and composure, ventured to speak.

'Who's there?' she asked.

'It's me! Me! Me!'

'Who's that?'

'Commissioner Passauf!'

Commissioner Passauf! The very man whose job they had been thinking of suppressing for the past ten years! So what was happening? Could the Burgundians have invaded Quiquendone as they had in the fourteenth century? Nothing less than an event of this importance could have affected to such a degree Commissioner Passauf, who was no wit less calm and phlegmatic than the burgomaster himself.

At a sign from van Tricasse – the worthy man would have been quite unable to utter a single word – the bar was pulled back, and the door half opened.

Commissioner Passauf swept into the hallway like a hurricane.

'What's the matter, commissioner?' asked Lotchè, a brave lass who never lost her head in the most serious circumstances.

'What's the matter!' replied Passauf, whose big round eyes were filled with real consternation. 'The matter is that I've just come from Dr Ox's house, where there was a reception, and there…'

'There?' said the councillor.

'There, I was witness to an altercation of a kind that… Burgomaster, they talked politics!'

'Politics!' repeated van Tricasse, running his fingers through his wig.

'Politics!' continued Commissioner Passauf, 'something that hasn't been seen for perhaps a hundred years in Quiquendone! And then the discussion became heated. The barrister, André Schut, and the doctor, Dominique Custos, laid into one another with such violence that they might end up calling each other out…'

'Calling each other out!' exclaimed the councillor. 'A duel! A duel in Quiquendone! So what did Barrister Schut and Dr Custos say to one another?'

'These were their very words. "Mr Barrister," the doctor said to his opponent, "you are going a bit too far, it seems to me, and you are not taking enough care to measure the effect of your words!" '

Burgomaster van Tricasse clasped his hands. The councillor went pale and dropped his lamp. The commissioner shook his head. Such a provocative exchange of words between two of the local notables!

'This Dr Custos,' murmured van Tricasse, 'really is a

dangerous, hot-headed man! Come, gentlemen!'

Upon which, Councillor Niklausse and the commissioner returned to the parlour with Burgomaster van Tricasse.

4

*In which Dr Ox reveals himself to be a physiologist
of the first order and a bold experimenter*

So who is this personage known by the strange name of
Dr Ox?

An eccentric, to be sure, but at the same time a bold
scientist, a physiologist whose works are known and esteemed
by scholars throughout Europe, a successful rival of figures
like Davy, Dalton, Bostock, Menzies, Godwin, Vierordt, and
all other such great minds who have brought physiology into
the front rank of the modern sciences.

Dr Ox was a man of middling girth, medium height, aged…
but we couldn't say exactly how old he was, any more than
we could tell you his nationality. In any case, it's not very
important. All you need to know is that he really was a strange
character, hot-blooded and impetuous, a veritable eccentric
who had escaped from a volume of Hoffmann stories and
formed a remarkable contrast, as you may well imagine, with
the inhabitants of Quiquendone. He had an unshakeable
confidence in himself and his doctrines. Always smiling,
walking with his head held high and swinging his shoulders in
a relaxed, free-and-easy manner, with a self-assured gaze, his
broad nostrils flaring, his huge mouth open to breathe in great
gulps of air – his whole figure was a pleasure to see. *He* was
alive all right, fully alive, well balanced in every part of his
machinery, always on the go, with quicksilver in his veins and
a spring in his step. So he could never stand still for long,
and kept breaking out into a torrent of words, while ceaselessly
gesticulating.

Was he rich, then, this Dr Ox, who had come to undertake

at his own expense the lighting of an entire town?

Probably, since he could permit himself such expenses, and this is the only reply we can make to such an indiscreet enquiry.

Dr Ox had arrived in Quiquendone five months previously, in the company of his assistant, who answered to the strange name of Gideon Ygène, a tall, gaunt, skinny fellow, a real beanpole, but no less full of life than his master.

So why, then, had Dr Ox undertaken to organise the town's lighting, and at his own expense? Why had he chosen those very same peaceable Quiquendonians, those most Flemish of folk, rather than others – and why did he want to endow their little town with the benefits of an incomparable system of lighting? Wasn't he using this as a pretext to attempt some great physiological experiment, performing it *in anima vili*? [6] What, in short, was this eccentric fellow up to? This is just what we don't know, as Dr Ox had no other confidant than his assistant Ygène, who, furthermore, obeyed him blindly.

To all appearances, at least, Dr Ox had promised to provide the town with lighting, which it did need, 'especially at nights', as Commissioner Passauf said. And so a factory for producing gas had been set up. The gasometers were ready to come into operation, and the gas pipes extending under the street paving were shortly due to be capped with gas burners in the public buildings and even in the private houses of certain allies of progress.

Van Tricasse, in his capacity as burgomaster, and Niklausse, in his capacity as councillor, together with numerous other notables, had thought it their duty to authorise the intro-duction of this modern lighting into their dwellings.

If the reader has not forgotten, it was said, during this long conversation between the councillor and the burgomaster, that the lighting of the town would be brought about not by the burning of common-or-garden carburetted hydrogen as produced by the distillation of coal, but instead by the use of that more modern gas, twenty times more brilliant – oxyhydric gas, produced by hydrogen and oxygen combined.

Now the doctor, a skilled chemist and a fine physicist, knew how to obtain this gas cheaply and plentifully, not by using sodium manganate, following the techniques employed by M. Tessié du Motay, but simply by decomposing water rendered slightly acidic by means of a battery made of new elements and invented by him. Hence there were no expensive substances, no platinum, no retorts, no inflammable fuel, no delicate apparatus of the kind necessary to produce the two gases in isolation. An electric current was passed through huge vats filled with water, and the liquid element was broken down into its two constituent parts, oxygen and hydrogen. The oxygen went one way; the hydrogen, twice as much in volume as its former associate, went another. Both were collected in separate reservoirs – an essential precaution, since if they had mixed, they would have produced a dreadful explosion, if exposed to a naked flame. Then, pipes were to lead them separately to the different gas burners, arranged in such a way as to prevent any explosion. Thereupon, a flame of remarkable brilliance would be produced, a flame whose brightness would rival that of electric light, which – as everyone knows – is, as shown by Casselmann's experiments, equal to the light of 1,171 candles: not one more and not one less.

It was certain that the town of Quiquendone would gain a splendid lighting system from this noble contrivance. But this was just what Dr Ox and his assistant were least concerned about, as we shall see later.

In fact, the very same day following the noisy appearance of Commissioner Passauf in the burgomaster's parlour, Gideon

Ygène and Dr Ox were both having a talk, in the office they shared, on the ground floor in the main building of the factory.

'Well now, Ygène, well now!' Dr Ox kept exclaiming, rubbing his hands together. 'You saw them yesterday, at our reception, those fine cold-blooded Quiquendonians who, if it's intensity of passion we're talking about, are halfway between sponges and coralligenous accretions! You saw them, quarrelling, uttering provocative words and making threatening gestures! Already transformed, morally and physically! And this is only the start! Just wait until you see what they do when we treat them with a high dose!'

'Too true, master,' replied Gideon Ygène, scratching his pointy noise with the tip of his index finger. 'The experiment has got off to a good start, and if I hadn't taken the precaution of closing the gas tap, I don't know what would have happened.'

'Did you hear that Barrister Schut and that Dr Custos?' continued Dr Ox. 'The words themselves weren't at all offensive, but in the mouth of a Quiquendonian they are as strong as the series of insults that the heroes of Homer hurl at each other before unsheathing their swords. Ah, these Flemish folk! You'll see what we'll turn them into one of these days.'

'We'll turn them into ungrateful wretches,' replied Gideon Ygène, in the tone of voice of a man who judges the human race at its proper worth.

'Terrific!' said the doctor. 'It doesn't matter much whether they're grateful to us or not, so long as our experiment succeeds!'

'But,' added the assistant with a cunning smile, 'shouldn't we be worried in case we produce such a high level of excitation in their respiratory apparatus that we affect the lungs of these worthy burghers of Quiquendone?'

'That's their problem!' replied Dr Ox. 'It's in the interests of science! What would you say if dogs or frogs refused to take part in vivisection?'

It is quite probable that, if frogs and dogs actually were consulted, these animals would voice quite a few objections to the experiments performed on them by vivisectors; but Dr Ox believed he had here found an irrefutable argument, and he breathed a huge sigh of satisfaction.

'After all, master, you're quite right,' replied Gideon Ygène in tones of conviction. 'We couldn't have found better subjects than these inhabitants of Quiquendone.'

'No, we could not,' said the doctor, emphasising every syllable.

'Have you taken their pulse?'

'A hundred times.'

'And what's the average pulse you've observed?'

'Less than fifty per minute. Just think: a town where for a whole century there hasn't been the shadow of a quarrel, where carters don't swear, where coachmen don't insult each other, where horses don't get restive, where dogs don't bark, where cats don't scratch! A town where the ordinary police court has nothing to do from one end of the year to the next! A town where people don't get passionate about anything, neither art, nor business! A town where gendarmes have become mythical creatures, and where nobody has been booked for a hundred years! A town, in short, where for three hundred years not a single punch or a slap has been exchanged! As you can see, Master Ygène, it can't last: we're going to change all that.'

'Perfect! Perfect!' replied the assistant, filled with enthusiasm. 'And what about the town air, master – have you analysed that?'

'Of course. Seventy-nine parts nitrogen and twenty-nine parts oxygen, carbonic acid and water vapour in varying quantities. Those are the usual proportions.'

'Good, doctor, good,' replied Master Ygène. 'The experiment will be a large-scale affair: it will prove decisive.'

'And if it is decisive,' added Dr Ox triumphantly, 'we will reform the world!'

5

*In which the burgomaster and councillor
pay a visit to Dr Ox, and what ensues*

Councillor Niklausse and Burgomaster van Tricasse discovered, at long last, what it was to experience a restless night. The serious event that had occurred in Dr Ox's house gave them real insomnia. What would be the consequences of the whole business? They couldn't imagine. Would they have to come to some decision? Would the municipal authority, represented by them, be forced to intervene? Would decrees be issued to prevent such a scandal ever happening again? All these doubts could not but disturb their indecisive natures. And so, the previous day, before they separated, the two notables had 'decided' to meet again the next day.

The next day, then, before dinner, Burgomaster van Tricasse betook himself to the house of Councillor Niklausse. He found his friend in a calmer frame of mind. He himself had regained his equilibrium.

'Nothing new?' asked van Tricasse.

'Nothing new since yesterday,' replied Niklausse.

'And the doctor, Dominique Custos?'

'I haven't heard a word about him, any more than about the barrister André Schut.'

After an hour's conversation that would fill a mere three lines, and that there is no point in relating, the councillor and the burgomaster had resolved to pay a visit to Dr Ox, so as to draw an explanation out of him without seeming to.

Contrary to all their habits, once this decision had been taken, the two notables made it a point of honour to carry it out immediately. They left the house and headed towards

Dr Ox's factory, situated outside the town, near the Oudenaarde Gate – precisely the same one whose tower was threatening to fall down.

The burgomaster and councillor didn't walk arm in arm, but strode along, *passibus aequis*, at a slow and solemn pace, which enabled them to advance at a rate of barely thirteen inches per second. This was, in any case, the ordinary gait of the citizens they administered, who, within living memory, had never seen anyone running through the streets of Quiquendone.

From time to time, at a calm and tranquil crossroads, or at the corner of some peaceful street, the two notables halted to greet people.

'Good day, burgomaster,' said one.

'Good day, my friend,' replied van Tricasse.

'No news, councillor?'

'No news,' replied Niklausse.

But it was easy to guess, from the astonishment on certain faces and the quizzical expression in certain eyes, that news of the previous day's altercation had spread through the town. Merely by noting the direction in which van Tricasse was heading, the most obtuse of the Quiquendonians would have surmised that the burgomaster was off engaged on serious business. The Custos and Schut affair was stirring every imagination, but people had not yet got around to taking sides with one or the other. This barrister and this doctor were, when all was said and done, both highly esteemed characters. Barrister Schut, who had never had an opportunity to plead in a town where solicitors and court ushers existed only as memories, had, in consequence, never lost a case. As for Dr Custos, he was an honourable practitioner who, following the example of his colleagues, cured his patients of all their illnesses, except the one they died from: a disagreeable habit that has been picked up, unfortunately, by all the members of the medical profession, whichever country they practise in.

Arriving at the Oudenaarde Gate, the councillor and the burgomaster took the precaution of making a small detour so as not to pass within the 'radius of fall' of the tower; then they gazed at it attentively.

'I think it will fall,' said van Tricasse.

'I think so too,' replied Niklausse.

'Unless we prop it up,' added van Tricasse. 'But do we *have* to prop it up? That is the question.'

'That, indeed, is the question,' replied Niklausse.

A few moments later, they presented themselves at the factory door.

'Is Dr Ox available?' they asked.

Dr Ox was always available for the leading authorities in the town, and the latter were immediately brought into the office of the celebrated physiologist.

Perhaps the two notables waited for a good hour before the doctor appeared. At least, we are justified in thinking so, as the burgomaster – and this was something that had never happened to him in his life before – showed a certain impatience, by which his companion, too, was not unaffected.

Dr Ox finally came in and apologised first for having kept these gentlemen waiting; but, what with the plan for a gasometer to approve, a connection to rectify… At all events, everything was going ahead. The pipes designed to carry oxygen had already been laid. Before a few months were up, the town would be equipped with splendid lighting. The two notables could already see the ends of the gas pipes emerging into the doctor's office.

Then the doctor enquired to what he owed the honour of a visit from the burgomaster and the councillor.

'We wanted to see you, doctor, just to see you,' replied van Tricasse. 'It's been a long time since we've had that pleasure. We don't go out much, in our good old town of Quiquendone. Every step we take, every action, is measured. Happy when nothing comes to disturb the uniformity...'

Niklausse was watching his friend. The latter had never had so much to say – at least not without taking ages over it, and interspersing his sentences with long pauses. It seemed to him that van Tricasse was expressing himself with a certain volubility that was far from habitual with him. Niklausse himself also felt, as it were, an irresistible itch to talk.

As for Dr Ox, he was watching the burgomaster closely with his cunning eyes.

Van Tricasse, who never conversed unless he was first comfortably settled down in a nice armchair, had on this occasion stood up. Some edgy excitability, quite unlike his usual temperament, had taken hold of him. He was not yet gesticulating, but it couldn't be long before he would do so. As for the councillor, he kept rubbing his calves and breathing in slow deep mouthfuls of air. His eyes gradually started to sparkle, and he had 'decided', all the same, to support – if need be – his trusty friend the burgomaster.

Van Tricasse had risen to his feet, taken a few steps, and then returned to stand in front of the doctor.

'And in how many months,' he said in a slightly deliberate tone of voice, 'in how many months do you say your work will be finished?'

'In three or four months, burgomaster,' replied Dr Ox.

'Three or four months – that's a long time!' said van Tricasse.

'Much too long!' added Niklausse who, unable to sit still any longer, had also risen.

'We need that length of time to finish our operation,' replied the doctor. 'The workers, whom we were obliged to choose from among the population of Quiquendone, aren't particularly expeditious.'

'What! Not expeditious?' exclaimed the burgomaster, who seemed to take this word as a personal insult.

'No, burgomaster,' replied Dr Ox with insistence. 'A French worker could perform in a single day the work of ten of the people in your charge. You know, they are pure Flemish fellows…'

'Flemish fellows?' exclaimed Councillor Niklausse, whose hands were starting to clench. 'And what exactly do you mean by that word, monsieur?'

'But… I mean the same pleasant thing as does everyone else,' replied the doctor with a smile.

'As for that, monsieur,' said the burgomaster, pacing up and down the office from one end to the other, 'I do not like those insinuations. The workers of Quiquendone are worth the workers in any other town in the world, do you know that? We don't need to look for role models in Paris or London! As for the work that concerns you, I will ask you kindly to speed up its execution. Our streets have been dug up so your gas pipes can be laid down, and this causes traffic hold-ups. Small businesses will start to complain, and as a responsible administrator I don't intend to incur criticisms that would be perfectly justifiable!'

Worthy burgomaster! He had spoken of small businesses, of traffic – and these words, unusual coming from him, did not blister his lips! Whatever could be happening inside him?

'In any case,' added Niklausse, 'the town can't manage without lighting for much longer.'

'But,' said the doctor, 'a town which has been happy to wait for eight or nine hundred years…'

'That is simply one more reason, monsieur,' replied the burgomaster, laying stress on every syllable. 'Times change and we must change with them. Progress is on the march and we don't want to be left behind! We want our streets to be lit within a month, or else you will pay a considerable fine for every day's delay. And whatever would happen if, in the darkness, a brawl were to break out?'

'He's right!' exclaimed Niklausse, 'it only takes a spark to set a Flemish man on fire! Flanders means flame!'

'And while we're on the subject,' said the burgomaster, interrupting his friend, 'it has been reported to us by the municipal chief of police, Commissioner Passauf, that there was an argument yesterday evening in your salon, doctor. Would one be mistaken in saying that it was a political argument?'

'No, it was indeed political, burgomaster,' replied Dr Ox, who could barely repress a sigh of satisfaction.

'And did an altercation not take place between Dr Dominique Custos and Barrister André Schut?'

'Yes, councillor, but the expressions that were exchanged were in no way serious.'

'In no way serious!' exclaimed the burgomaster, 'in no way serious – when one man says to another that he is not taking enough care to measure the effect of his words! But what kind of a man are you, monsieur? Don't you know that in Quiquendone such remarks are quite enough to lead to extremely regrettable consequences? Monsieur, if you or anyone else were to permit themselves to speak to *me* like that…'

'Or me!' added Councillor Niklausse.

As they uttered these words in voices full of menace, the two notables, their arms folded, their hair bristling, were staring across at Dr Ox, ready to make him regret it if a gesture – no, not even a gesture, a single glance from him – were to suggest that he had any hostile intent.

But the doctor didn't flinch.

'In any case, monsieur,' continued the burgomaster, 'I intend to hold you responsible for what happens in your house. I answer for the tranquillity of this town, and I will not have it disturbed. The events that occurred yesterday will not happen again – or else I shall carry out my duty, monsieur. Do you hear me? Answer me, then, monsieur!'

As he uttered these words, the burgomaster, in the grip of an extraordinary agitation, had started to raise his voice to the pitch of anger. He was furious, this worthy van Tricasse, and he could certainly be heard outside. Finally, beside himself, seeing that the doctor refused to respond to his provocations, he said:

'Come, Niklausse.'

And, slamming the door with a violence which shook the house, the burgomaster dragged the councillor after him.

Little by little, once they had walked twenty steps or so in the countryside, the worthy notables calmed down. Their pace slowed, their expression changed. The flush on their faces began to fade. Having been red, it turned pink.

And a quarter of an hour after leaving the factory, van Tricasse was saying gently to Councillor Niklausse:

'He's a thoroughly nice fellow, that Dr Ox! I always look forward to seeing him.'

6

In which Frantz Niklausse and Suzel van Tricasse
make a few plans for the future

Our readers know that the burgomaster had a daughter,
Mlle Suzel. But, however perspicacious they may be, they
cannot possibly have guessed that Councillor Niklausse had a
son, M. Frantz. And, even if they had guessed it, nothing could
have permitted them to imagine that Frantz was Suzel's fiancé.
We will add that these two young people were made for each
other, and that they loved each other in the way people love
each other in Quiquendone.

You must not get the impression that young hearts did not
beat in this exceptional city. It's just that they beat with
a certain slowness. People got married here, just as in all
the towns in the world, but they took their time. The future
husband and wife, before committing themselves to those
terrible bonds, wanted to study one another, and these studies
lasted for at least ten years, just like at school. It was rare that
anyone 'passed' their exams before that time.

Yes, ten years! They paid court to each other for ten years!
Is it *really* too long, when it's a matter of being bound together
for life? People study for ten years to become engineers
or doctors, barristers or councillors in a *préfecture* – and
do you think anyone can acquire the knowledge necessary
to be a husband in less time? This is unthinkable and,
whether through temperament or reasoned reflection, the
Quiquendonians are in our view quite right to extend their
studies this long. When you see that in other towns – warm-
blooded, uninhibited towns – marriages are contracted
in a few months, you can only shrug your shoulders and

decide without delay to send your boys to day school and your daughters to boarding school in Quiquendone.

Only one marriage that had been contracted in a mere two years could be pointed to in the past half-century – and that one had turned out to be a failure!

So Frantz Niklausse loved Suzel van Tricasse, but in a placid way, as you would expect when you have ten years ahead of you to win your beloved. Every week, just once a week and at an agreed time, Frantz would come to fetch Suzel, and go off with her to the banks of the Vaar. He took care to bring his fishing rod, and Suzel made sure she never forgot her embroidery, in which her pretty fingers brought together the most unlikely combinations of flowers.

This is the place to say that Frantz was a young man of twenty-two, that a light peachy down was starting to appear on his cheeks, and finally that his voice had only just gone down an octave.

As for Suzel, she was blonde and pink. She was seventeen and wasn't at all averse to fishing – a strange pastime, though: one that forces you to pit your wits against those of a barbel. But Frantz loved it. This hobby suited his temperament. He was as patient as one can be, happy to follow with a somewhat dreamy eye the cork float that trembled in the stream, and quite capable of waiting until, after a six-hour session, a medium-sized barbel, taking pity on him, finally agreed to let itself get caught; then he was happy, but he managed to contain his joy.

On this particular day, the future husband and wife, or fiancés, one might say, were sitting on a verdant river bank. The limpid Vaar was rippling along a few feet below them. Suzel was nonchalantly threading her needle through her embroidery. Frantz automatically pulled his line from left to right, then he let it float back down the current from right to left. The barbels were making capricious ripples in the water, that criss-crossed all around the float, while the hook dangled, at a loose end, in the empty lower levels of the water.

From time to time, Frantz would say, 'I think I've got a bite, Suzel,' without even lifting his eyes to look at the young girl.

'Do you think so, Frantz?' Suzel would reply, looking up for a moment from her work to follow with an intent eye her fiancé's line.

'Ah, no,' resumed Frantz. 'I thought I could feel a slight tug. I was wrong.'

'You'll get a bite, Frantz,' replied Suzel in her pure, gentle voice. 'But don't forget to hook him in quickly. You're always a few seconds late, and the barbel takes advantage to escape.'

'Would you like to take my rod, Suzel?'

'I'd love to, Frantz.'

'Give me your embroidery, then. We'll see if I'm any niftier with the needle than with the hook.'

And the young girl took over the rod, her hand trembling, and the young man threaded the needle through the mesh of the tapestry. And for hours on end they would exchange gentle words in this way, and their hearts skipped a beat when the float quivered on the water. Ah! May they never forget those delightful hours during which, sitting next to one another, they listened to the murmur of the river!

That day, the sun was already low down on the horizon and, despite the combined talents of Suzel and Frantz, 'the fish just weren't biting'. The barbels hadn't showed any compassion, and were laughing at the two young people – who didn't feel in the slightest put out.

'We'll have better luck next time, Frantz,' said Suzel, when the young fisherman stuck his still virginal fishhook back into his pinewood board.

'Let's hope so, Suzel,' replied Frantz.

Then the two of them, walking side by side, set out on their way home, without exchanging a word, as silent as their shadows, which lengthened before them. Suzel saw herself grow tall, tall, beneath the slanting rays of the setting sun. Frantz appeared thin, thin, like the long rod he was holding.

They reached the burgomaster's house. Green tufts of grass framed the gleaming cobbles, and nobody would have even thought of pulling them out, as they provided an upholstered surface for the street and muffled the sound of people's footsteps.

Just as the door was about to open, Frantz thought it was the time to say to his fiancée:

'You know, Suzel, the great day is coming.'

'Yes, it's coming, Frantz!' replied the young girl, lowering her long eyelids.

'Yes,' said Frantz, 'in five or six years…'

'Goodbye, Frantz,' said Suzel.

'Goodbye, Suzel,' replied Frantz.

And, once the door had shut behind her, Frantz continued, at an even and tranquil pace, to make his way to the house of Councillor Niklausse.

7

In which the andantes become allegros,
and the allegros become vivaces

The stir caused by the incident involving Barrister Schut and Dr Custos had died down. The affair had been without consequences. So it was permitted to hope that Quiquendone would return to its habitual apathy, which an inexplicable event had momentarily disturbed.

Meanwhile, the laying down of the pipes that would bring oxyhydric gas to the main buildings in town was proceeding apace. The main pipes and branch pipes were starting gradually to ramify under the streets of Quiquendone. But the burners were still missing; as they were so delicate to manufacture, it had been necessary to have them made abroad. Dr Ox was everywhere at once; his assistant Ygène and himself didn't waste a moment, urging on the workers, finishing off the delicate mechanism of the gasometer, and keeping fuelled, night and day, the gigantic batteries that decomposed the water under the influence of a powerful electric current. Yes! The doctor was already manufacturing his gas, even though the distribution system was not yet finished; which, between you and me, ought to have appeared really rather strange. But before very long – at least, people had every reason to hope – before very long, in the town theatre, Dr Ox would inaugurate the splendours of his new lighting.

Quiquendone did indeed possess a theatre – a fine building, upon my word, whose interior and exterior arrangement recalled every possible style. It was at one and the same time Byzantine, Roman, Gothic, Renaissance, with semicircular doors, ogival windows, flamboyant rose windows, fantastic pinnacle turrets – in a word, it was a specimen of all genres: half Parthenon, half grand Parisian café. This shouldn't astonish us; having been begun under Burgomaster Ludwig van Tricasse in 1175, it was completed only in 1837 under Burgomaster Natalis van Tricasse. It had taken seven hundred years to build, and it had conformed to the architectural fashion of each successive period. Never mind! It was a fine building, whose Roman pillars and Byzantine domes didn't clash too much with oxyhydric gas lighting.

Pretty much all sorts of things were put on at the Quiquendone theatre: comedy, opera, ballet, comic opera, vaudeville, and even the operettas of Hervé and Offenbach. Yes, these two great masters, the honour of the second half of the nineteenth century, had infiltrated the town walls of Quiquendone. But it has to be said that neither the German nor the Frenchman would have recognised *L'Oeil crevé* or *La Belle Hélène*, so greatly had their *movements* been changed.[7]

The fact was that, as nothing was ever done quickly in Quiquendone, theatrical works had been forced to tailor themselves to the temperament of the Quiquendonians. Although the doors of the theatre usually opened at four o'clock and closed at ten, it simply never happened that, during those six hours, they ever got through more than two acts. *Robert le Diable, Les Huguenots, William Tell*, habitually took up a good three evenings, so slow was the performance of these masterpieces.[8] The vivaces, in the theatre of Quiquendone, sauntered along like real adagios. The allegros were dragged out slowly, slowly. The hemidemisemiquavers were scarcely equal to ordinary semibreves in any other country. The most rapid roulades, performed in the taste of the Quiquendonians, had the heavy tread of a plainchant hymn. The nonchalant trills grew languid and stiff, so as not to offend the ears of the dilettanti. One example will say it all: Figaro's lively aria, his entry in the first act of *The Barber of Seville*, was taken at a beat of thirty-three on the metronome and lasted for fifty-eight minutes – when, that is, the singer was really prepared to whizz through his part.

As you can well imagine, the artistes who came from outside town had been obliged to conform to this fashion; but, since they were well paid, they didn't complain, and faithfully followed the baton of the conductor who, in the allegros, never beat more than eight bars per minute.

And yet, what applause greeted these artistes, who delighted the spectators of Quiquendone, and never let them feel bored or tired! They clapped their hands together regularly, at rather frequent intervals, which the reviews in the newspapers translated as *frenzied applause*; and on more than one occasion, if the auditorium didn't collapse under the cries of 'bravo!', it was only because, in the twelfth century, the builders didn't skimp on either cement or stone when laying the foundations.

Furthermore, so as not to overexcite those enthusiastic Flemish temperaments, the theatre put on a performance only once a week, which enabled the actors to deepen their roles, and the spectators to digest the beauties of these masterpieces of the dramatic art at greater leisure.

Now, things had been that way for a long time. Foreign artistes were in the habit of contracting an engagement with the director of the Quiquendone theatre whenever they wanted to take a rest from their exertions on other stages, and it seemed as if nothing would ever modify these inveterate customs, when, a fortnight after the Schut-Custos affair, an unexpected incident came along to spread renewed unease through the population.

It was a Saturday: opera day. The time had still not come, as you might have expected, to inaugurate the new lighting. No: the pipes now reached the auditorium, it was true, but, for the reason mentioned above, the gas burners had still not been fixed, and the candles of the chandelier still shed their gentle light on the numerous spectators crowding the theatre. The doors had been opened to the public at one o'clock in the afternoon, and at four the auditorium was half full. At one moment there had been a queue winding as far as the other end of the Place Saint-Ernuph, outside the shop of the chemist, Josse Liefrinck. This swarm of eager spectators suggested there was going to be a fine performance.

'Will you be going to the theatre this evening?' the councillor had asked the burgomaster that very same morning.

'I certainly will,' van Tricasse had replied, 'and I'm going to take Mme van Tricasse, as well as our daughter Suzel and our dear Aunty Némance, who are both very keen on good music.'

'Will Mlle Suzel be coming?' asked the councillor.

'She probably will, Niklausse.'

'Then my son Frantz will be one of the first to join the queue,' replied Niklausse.

'A passionate boy, Niklausse,' replied the burgomaster sagaciously. 'A bit hot-headed! You ought to keep an eye on that young man.'

'He's in love, van Tricasse, he's in love with your charming Suzel.'

'Well in that case, Niklausse, he'll marry her. Since we're agreed on the marriage, what more can he ask for?'

'He's not asking for anything, van Tricasse, he's not asking for anything, the dear boy! But let's just say – and this is all I *will* say about it – that he won't be the last to collect his ticket from the kiosk!'

'Ah! Passionate, high-spirited youth!' replied the burgomaster, smiling at his own past. 'We were exactly the same, my esteemed councillor! We too have known love! We too have joined the queue in our time! So, I'll see you this evening then. By the way, do you know that he's a great artiste, this Fioravanti! And what a reception he's been given within our walls! It will be a long time before he forgets the applause of Quiquendone!'

The man he was referring to was the famous tenor Fioravanti who, with his virtuoso talent, his consummate method, and his fine voice, aroused real enthusiasm among the town's music lovers.

For three weeks, Fioravanti had been scoring a real hit with *Les Huguenots*. The first act, performed in the taste of the Quiquendonians, had filled out an entire evening in the first week of the month. Another evening in the second week, drawn out by countless andantes, had earned the celebrated singer a veritable ovation. The success had been even greater with the third act of Meyerbeer's masterpiece. But it was in the fourth act that people were really looking forward to hearing Fioravanti, and this fourth act was due to be performed this very evening, before an impatient audience. Ah! That duet between Raoul and Valentine, that hymn of love for two voices, conveyed in expansive sighs, that stretto in which there is a succession of crescendos, stringendos, accelerandos, and più crescendos, the whole piece sung slowly, compendiously, interminably! Ah, what delight!

So, at four o'clock, the auditorium was full. The boxes, the orchestra, the pit, all were overflowing. In the stage boxes were ranged Burgomaster van Tricasse, Mlle van Tricasse, Mme van Tricasse and the good-natured Aunty Némance in an apple-green bonnet; then, not far away from them, Councillor

Niklausse and his family, not forgetting the amorous Frantz. One could also see the families of Dr Custos, Barrister Schut, Honoré Syntax, the chief judge, and Soutman (Norbert), the director of the insurance company, and the fat banker Collaert, who was mad about German music, something of a virtuoso himself, and the tax collector Rupp, and the director of the academy, Jérôme Resh, and the civil commissioner, and countless others from among the town's notables – so many that it would be impossible to enumerate them all here without exhausting the reader's patience.

Ordinarily, as they waited for the curtain to be raised, the Quiquendonians were in the habit of remaining silent, some of them reading their newspapers, the others exchanging a few words in a low voice; some made their way to their seats without noise and without haste, while others glanced with a half-extinguished glitter in their eyes at the attractive beauties on prominent display in the circle.

But, that evening, an observer would have noted that, even before the curtain went up, an unaccustomed animation had filled the auditorium. You could see people gesticulating emphatically who never usually gesticulated at all. The ladies' fans were fluttering with a quite abnormal rapidity. A more vivacious air seemed to have filled all their bosoms. They were breathing more deeply. Eyes were shining and, to be quite honest, shining almost as brightly as the flames of the chandelier, which seemed to shed on the auditorium an unaccustomed dazzle. It was true: you could see more clearly than usual, even though the lighting had not been turned up. Ah! If only Dr Ox's new apparatuses had been working; but they weren't yet in operation.

Finally the orchestra is in its seats, in full strength. The first violinist has passed between the desks to give a modest A to his colleagues. The string instruments, the wind instruments, the percussion instruments, have all tuned up. The conductor is merely awaiting the bell so he can beat the first bar.

The bell rings out. The fourth act begins. The allegro appassionato of the entr'acte is played, as is the habit, with a majestic slowness which would have made the illustrious Meyerbeer jump out of his skin, and whose full majesty is savoured by the music lovers of Quiquendone.

But soon the conductor feels he has lost control of his performers. He finds it difficult to hold them back – when they are usually so obedient, so calm. The wind instruments have a tendency to push the rhythm forward, and he has to rein them in with a firm hand, since otherwise they'd get ahead of the strings – which, from the harmonic point of view, would produce a regrettable effect. The bassoonist himself, the son of the chemist Josse Liefrinck, such a well brought-up young man, is starting to get carried away.

Meanwhile, Valentine has begun her recitative:

'*I am alone at home…*'

But she's started to pick up speed. The conductor and all his musicians follow her – perhaps without realising it – in her cantabile, which ought to be beaten quite slowly, like the twelve-eight it is. When Raoul appears in the door at the back of the stage, between the moment when Valentine goes to him and when she hides him in the bedroom next door, less than a quarter of an hour goes by – whereas previously, in accordance with the tradition of the theatre of Quiquendone, this recitative thirty-seven bars long lasted for a good thirty-seven minutes.

Saint-Bris, Nevers, Tavannes and the Catholic noblemen

have come on stage, a bit too quickly perhaps. Allegro pomposo is what the composer indicated on his score. The orchestra and the noblemen are indeed going allegro, but not in the slightest pomposo, and in the ensemble piece, that magisterial scene including the oath and the blessing of the daggers, the statutory allegro is no longer being played at a moderate tempo. Singers and musicians slip their leash and make a dash for it. The conductor isn't even trying to keep them back. In any case, the audience doesn't want him to – quite the opposite: you can feel that he is being swept along too, that he's caught up in the movement, and that this movement expresses the longings of his soul:

> *From renewed warfare and an impious band,*
> *Will you, like me, deliver our fair land?*

They make their promises and swear their oaths. Nevers hardly has time to protest and to sing that 'among his ancestors, there are only soldiers, and not one murderer'. He is arrested. The municipal officials and the magistrates come running up and rapidly swear 'to strike all at once'. Saint-Bris smashes through the recitative summoning the Catholics to vengeance as if it were a flimsy gate, at a veritable two-four tempo. The three monks, carrying baskets with white scarves, dash through the door at the back of Nevers' apartment, paying no attention to the stage directions, which require them to advance slowly. Already all those present have drawn their swords and their daggers, which the three monks bless with a wave of their hands. The sopranos, the tenors and the bass launch into the allegro furioso uttering cries of rage, and turn a dramatic six-eight into the six-eight of a quadrille. Then they leave, bellowing:

'At midnight,
Keeping quiet!
It is God's will!
Yes,
At midnight.'

At this moment, the audience is on its feet. There is a frenzy in the boxes, the pit, the circle. It looks as if all the spectators are about to rush forward onto the stage, Burgomaster van Tricasse at their head, so as to join the conspirators and anni-hilate the Huguenots – even though they share the religious opinions of the latter. They applaud, call the actors back, greet them with shouts and cheers! Aunty Némance feverishly waves her apple-green bonnet. The lamps in the auditorium shed a warm glow…

Raoul, instead of slowly lifting the drapery, tears it proudly in two and finds himself face to face with Valentine.

Finally! It's time for the great duo, and it's taken at an allegro vivace. Raoul doesn't wait for Valentine's questions and Valentine doesn't wait for Raoul's answers. The really lovely passage:

Danger presses
And time is short…

becomes one of those rapid pieces in two-four which have made Offenbach so famous, when he makes some conspira-tors or other dance around. The andante amoroso:

You have said it!
Yes, you love me!

is now nothing but a vivace furioso, and the cello in the orchestra is no longer bothering to try and mimic the inflections of the singer's voice, as is indicated in the master's score. In vain does Valentine exclaim:

> '*Prolong it even more,*
> *Prolong my heart's ineffable slumber!*'

Raoul *can't* prolong it! You sense that an unaccustomed fire is devouring him. His Bs and his Cs, above his range, have a fearful edge to them. He flings himself about, gesticulates, he is aflame…

The bell rings from the bell-tower; but what a breathless bell it is! The bell-ringer who is ringing it has obviously lost all self-control. It is a dreadful tocsin, locked in a violent struggle to make itself heard above the furious sounds of the orchestra.

Finally the stretto that is to bring this magnificent act to a conclusion:

> *No more love, and no more ecstasy!*
> *Oh, this remorse that so oppresses me!*

that the composer indicates as an allegro con moto, gallops headlong into a prestissimo. It is like an express train rattling along. The bell starts pealing out again. Valentine falls in a swoon. Raoul leaps out of the window!…

Just in time, too. The orchestra, now really intoxicated, couldn't have continued. The conductor's baton has been reduced to a stick broken on the prompter's desk. The strings of the violins are broken and their necks wrung! In his fury, the timpanist has burst his timpani! The bass player is perched on top of his resonant edifice! The principal clarinettist has swallowed the reed of his ridiculous instrument, and the second oboist is chewing *his* reed in his teeth! The slide of the trombone is buckled and bent, and, finally, the unfortunate horn player can't get his hand out of the bell of his horn, where he stuck it in much too deep!

And as for the audience!... The audience, panting and inflamed, is gesticulating and howling! All their faces are red as if a fire were blazing within their bodies! They jostle and shove to get out as fast as they can, the men without their hats, the women without their coats! They elbow each other in the corridors, they form a crush at the doors, they quarrel, they fight! No more authorities! No more burgomaster! All are equal in this infernal overexcitement...

And, a few moments later, when everyone is out in the street, they each fall back into their habitual calm and peaceably return to their homes, with only a confused memory of what they have experienced.

The fourth act of *Les Huguenots*, which used to last six hours by the clock, and had started, on that particular evening, at half past four, was over by twelve minutes to five.

It had lasted eighteen minutes!

8

In which the traditional, solemn German
waltz changes into a whirlwind

But while it is true that the spectators, on leaving the theatre, had regained their habitual calm, and peacefully made their way home with no trace of their experience other than a passing stupor, they had nonetheless been subjected to an extraordinary sense of intense excitement and, feeling exhausted, dead-beat, as if they had overindulged at table, they collapsed into their beds.

Now, the following day, each of them had as it were a flashback to what had happened to them the day before. One was missing his hat, lost in the brawl, another had lost a flap of his jacket, torn in the mêlée; one woman had lost her fine prunella shoe, another the cloak she wore on special occasions. Memory returned to these upstanding middle-class people and, with memory, a certain shame at their indescribable high spirits. It appeared to them as an orgy in which they had unconsciously played the part of the protagonists! They didn't talk about it; they preferred not to think about it.

But the most dumbfounded person in the whole town was in fact Burgomaster van Tricasse. The following morning, when he awoke, he couldn't find his wig. Lotchè had looked everywhere. Nothing. The wig had been left on the battlefield. As for having the town trumpeter, Jean Mistrol, advertise its loss – no: it was better to sacrifice one's hairpiece than to make an exhibition of oneself, when one had the honour to be the principal magistrate in the community.

These were the worthy van Tricasse's reflections, as he lay stretched out under his blankets, his body tired and aching, his head heavy, his tongue furred, his lungs burning. He felt not the slightest desire to get up – quite the opposite – and his brain worked harder this whole morning than it had done for perhaps forty years. The honourable magistrate went over in his head every individual moment of that inexplicable performance. He compared it with the events which had recently occurred that evening at Dr Ox's. He tried to find the reasons behind this bizarre excitability which, on two occasions, had manifested itself among the most dependable of the citizens under his charge.

'Whatever can be happening?' he kept asking himself. 'What spirit of giddy delirium has taken hold of my peaceable town of Quiquendone? Are we all going to go off our heads, and will the town have to be turned into a huge asylum? After all, there we all were yesterday: notables, councillors, judges, barristers, doctors, academicians – and all of us, if my memory is correct, all of us fell prey to this attack of wild mania! Whatever could there have been in that infernal music? It's inexplicable! And yet I hadn't eaten or drunk anything which might have produced such a state of overexcitement in myself! No, yesterday all I had for dinner was a slice of overdone veal, a few spoonfuls of mashed spinach, a dish of floating islands and two glasses of weak beer diluted with pure water – nothing that would go to my head! No. There's something I can't explain and as, after all, I'm responsible for the actions of those in my charge, I will set up an enquiry.'

But the enquiry, approved by the town council, produced no results. If the facts were self-evident, the causes escaped the sagacity of the magistrates. In any case, calm had been restored in everyone's mind, and with calm came a forgetting of all the excesses they had committed. The newspapers of the locality did not so much as mention them, and the review of the performance, which appeared in the *Quiquendone Recorder*, made no allusion to the way a whole auditorium had succumbed to such feverish behaviour.

And yet, though the town fell back into its habitual impassivity, though it became once more, in appearance, as Flemish as it had been before, there was a feeling that, basically, the character and temperament of its inhabitants was gradually changing. You could have truly said, as did Dr Dominique Custos, that 'they were starting to develop a nervous system'.

We should make things clear, however. This indisputable and undisputed change occurred only in certain conditions. When the Quiquendonians walked through the streets of the town, out in the fresh air, in the squares, or along the Vaar, they were still those fine, cold and methodical folk that they had been before. The same applied when they kept themselves shut in their homes, some of them engaged in manual labour and others in mental labour, the latter doing nothing and the former not thinking. Their private lives were silent, inert, vegetative as they had been for so long. They did not quarrel, or scold each other in their households; there was no acceleration in their heartbeats, no overexcitement of their spinal cords. Their average pulse remained what it had been in the good old days: between fifty and fifty-two per minute.

But (and this was an absolutely inexplicable phenomenon, which would have baffled the sagacity of the most ingenious physiologists of the period) while the inhabitants of Quiquendone were quite unchanged in their private lives, they were on the contrary undergoing a visible transformation in the life they lived together – in those relations between individuals attendant on communal life.

So, if they met together in a public building, it 'didn't work out like it used to', to use the expression of Commissioner Passauf. In the stock exchange, in the town hall, in the chamber of the Academy, in council sessions and in scholarly assemblies, a sort of revitalisation occurred, and a strange overexcitability soon took hold of those present. After an hour, relations between them were already strained. After two hours, the discussion had degenerated into a dispute. Tempers flared, and they started attacking each other personally. Even at church, during the sermon, the faithful could not listen in a cool and collected way to Minister van Stabel – who, indeed, started making sweeping gestures from his pulpit and delivered severer admonitions to them than usual. Eventually this state of things led to even greater altercations than the one between Dr Custos and Barrister Schut; but they never required the intervention of authority, since once the parties in the quarrel had returned home, they calmed down and forgot all about the insults they had given and received.

Nonetheless, this strange fact had made no impression on minds absolutely incapable of recognising what was going on within themselves. A single person in the town, the very same one whose job the council had been thinking of suppressing for thirty years, the civil commissioner, Michel Passauf, had noticed that this overexcitement, while absent from private houses, manifested itself rapidly in public buildings, and he asked himself, not without a certain anxiety, what would happen when this arousal spread as far as the homes of the burghers, and when the epidemic – this was the word he used, appropriately enough – spilled over into the streets of the town. *Then* insults would not be forgotten, peace and quiet would have vanished, the delirium would no longer be merely sporadic but would have permanently inflamed everyone's temper, and this would inevitably set the Quiquendonians violently against one another.

'And then what will happen?' Commissioner Passauf wondered fearfully. 'How can those savage outbreaks of fury be stopped? How can those goaded temperaments be kept in check? In such circumstances, my office will no longer be a sinecure, and the council will really have to double my salary... unless I am forced to arrest *myself*... for a breach of the peace and public disorder!'

And these all-too-justified fears started to come true. From the stock exchange, the church, the theatre, the town hall, the Academy, and the covered market, the disease invaded the homes of individuals – less than a fortnight after that terrible performance of *Les Huguenots*.

It was in the home of the banker, Collaert, that the first symptoms of the epidemic appeared.

This wealthy personage was giving a ball, or at least a dance, for the town's notables. He had, a few months previously, floated a loan of thirty thousand francs which had been three-quarters subscribed and, to mark this financial success, he had opened his salons and thrown a party for his compatriots.

Everyone knows what these Flemish receptions are like: pure and tranquil occasions on which beer and soft drinks, prodigally served, are the only drinks provided. A few conversations on the weather, the appearance of the harvests, the fine state of the gardens, the tending of the flowers and more particularly the tulips; from time to time a slow, stiff dance, like a minuet, sometimes a waltz, but one of those German waltzes that involve no more than one and a half turns to the minute, and during which the waltzers hold one another in an embrace as distant as their arms will possibly permit – such was the usual demeanour of those balls which

Quiquendone high society used to frequent. Even the polka, after having been set to a four-four time, had made a real effort to gain acceptance here; but the dancers could never keep up with the orchestra, however slowly the tempo was beat, and the attempt had been perforce abandoned.

These peaceful gatherings, at which young men and women enjoyed themselves in a measured and decent fashion, had never led to any unpleasantness. So why was it that on that particular evening, at the home of the banker Collaert, the soft drinks and sugared water seemed to transform themselves into heady wines, sparkling champagne, and incendiary glasses of punch? Why, around the middle of the party, did a sort of inexplicable intoxication overcome all the guests? Why did the minuet slip into a saltarello? Why did the musicians in the orchestra start to speed up? Why was it that, just as in the theatre, the candles gleamed with an unaccustomed dazzle? What electric current invaded the banker's salons? What caused the couples to draw closer to one another, their arms to clasp one another in a more convulsive embrace, and a few daring steps to distinguish the *cavaliers seuls* during the fourth figure of this quadrille that had once been so grave, so solemn, so majestic, so *comme il faut*?

Alas! What Oedipus would have been able to answer all these insoluble questions? Commissioner Passauf, who was present at the occasion, could clearly see the gathering storm, but he could not hold it at bay, he could not flee it, and he felt a kind of intoxication rising to his brain. All his physiological faculties and all his passionate impulses grew in intensity. He was seen, several times over, pouncing on the sweets and snaffling the contents of every tray as if he had just come off a long diet.

During this time, the ball became increasingly animated.

A prolonged murmur, like a muffled hum, escaped from every breast. People were dancing, really dancing. Their feet shimmied and capered along with a growing frenzy. Their faces gleamed like carbuncles. The general ferment reached new heights of intensity.

And when the orchestra struck up the waltz from *Der Freischütz*, when the hired musicians launched with feverish gesticulations into this waltz, so German and so slow in tempo – ah! it was no longer a waltz, it was a demented whirlwind, a dizzying vortex, a gyration worthy of being conducted by some Faust, beating time with a burning brand from hell! Then a gallop, an infernal gallop, lasting an hour, without anyone being able to slow it down or bring it to a pause, dragged everyone along in its train as it rapidly twisted and turned through rooms, salons, antechambers and staircases, from cellar to attic of this opulent abode: young men, young women, fathers, mothers, individuals of every age, of every weight, of every sex: the fat banker Collaert, and Mme Collaert, and the councillors, and the magistrates, and the chief judge, and Niklausse, and Mme van Tricasse, and Burgomaster van Tricasse, and Commissioner Passauf himself, who could never remember who had been his waltz partner during that night of intoxication!

But 'she' could never forget *him*. And ever since that day, 'she' sees in her dreams, again and again, the ardent commissioner clasping her in a passionate embrace! And 'she' was – dear old Aunty Némance!

In which Dr Ox and his assistant Ygène
merely say a few words to each other

'Well, Ygène?'

'Well, master, everything's ready! They've finished laying down the pipes.'

'Good! Now we're going to operate on the grand scale: let's get to work on the masses!'

*In which the reader will see that the epidemic invaded
the entire town and what effects it produced*

In the following months, the malady, instead of fading away, simply spread ever further. From individual homes the epidemic spread into the streets. The town of Quiquendone was no longer recognisable.

An even more extraordinary phenomenon than those which had been noticed hitherto was the way that not only the animal kingdom, but even the vegetable kingdom itself did not escape this influence.

In the ordinary run of things, epidemics affect special groups. Those which afflict human beings don't affect animals, those which afflict animals don't affect vegetables. No one has ever seen a horse infected by smallpox, nor a human being by bovine disease. Sheep don't catch diseases that affect potatoes. But in this case, all the laws of nature seemed to have been turned topsy-turvy. Not only had the character, the temperament, and the ideas of the male and female inhabitants of Quiquendone been modified, but their domesticated animals – dogs and cats, oxen or horses, donkeys or goats – fell prey to this epidemic influence, as if their habitual environment had changed. The plants themselves started to 'live it up', if we may be permitted to use this expression.

Indeed, in gardens, vegetable plots and orchards, extremely curious symptoms became apparent. Climbing plants climbed more boldly. Tufting plants 'tufted' more vigorously. Shrubs became trees. Hardly had seeds been sown than already they were showing their little green shoots, and, in the same period of time, they grew as many inches as, once upon a time, even in the most favourable circumstances, they had grown in fractions of an inch. Asparaguses reached a height of two feet; artichokes became as big as melons, melons as big as gourds, gourds as big as pumpkins, pumpkins as big as the bell in the belfry – and good heavens, this bell was nine feet in diameter! Cabbages were bushes and mushrooms umbrellas.

Fruit did not wait for long before following the vegetables' example. It took two people to eat a strawberry and four to eat a pear. The bunches of grapes were as huge as that phenomenal bunch so admirably painted by Poussin in his *The Grapes of the Promised Land*!

The same was true of the flowers: the expansive violets filled the air with the most intense perfumes; the exaggeratedly big roses were resplendent in the brightest of colours; in a mere few days, the lilacs formed almost unbelievable thickets; geraniums, daisies, dahlias, camelias and rhododendrons invaded the garden paths and started to choke one another! A bill hook wasn't enough to keep them cut back. And the tulips, those darling members of the Liliaceae that are the pride and joy of the Flemish – what emotion they inspired in the breasts of their devotees! The worthy van Bistrom almost fell over backwards one day, on seeing in his garden a mere *Tulipa gesnerana* grown to an enormous, monstrous, gigantic size, its calyx providing a nest for a whole family of robins!

The entire town flocked to see this phenomenal flower, and dubbed it with the name *Tulipa quiquendonia*.

But alas! while these plants, fruits, and flowers grew as you watched them, while all the vegetation contrived to take on colossal proportions, while the intensity of their colours and scents intoxicated your nose and eyes, they did, conversely, soon wither. The air which they absorbed consumed them rapidly, and they soon died, exhausted, withered, ravaged.

Such was the fate of the celebrated tulip, which drooped and wilted after a few days of splendour!

The same was soon true of domestic animals, from the pet dog to the pig in the sty, from the canary in its cage to the turkeycock in the farmyard.

It is worth saying that these animals, ordinarily, were no less phlegmatic than their masters. Cats and dogs vegetated rather than lived. They never quivered with pleasure or shook with anger. Their tails didn't wag any more than if they had been made of bronze. From time immemorial no one could remember an animal lashing out with tooth or claw. As for rabid dogs, they were viewed as imaginary beasts, to be set alongside griffins and others in the menagerie of the Apocalypse.

But, during those few months, the least incidents of which we are trying to record, what a change! Cats and dogs started to show their teeth and their claws. After repeated attacks, there were several executions. For the first time, a horse was seen to take the bit in its teeth and bolt through the streets of Quiquendone; an ox charged, horns lowered, at one of its fellow creatures, a donkey rolled over, legs in the air, on the Place Saint-Ernuph, uttering braying noises that had ceased to have anything 'animal-like' about them, and a sheep (a *sheep!*), valiantly defended against the butcher's knife the mutton chops it carried inside itself!

Burgomaster van Tricasse was obliged to issue by-laws to control the domestic animals that, seized with madness, were making the streets of Quiquendone unsafe.

But alas! if animals were mad, human beings were no saner. No age was spared by the scourge.

Babies – who had hitherto been so easy to bring up – rapidly became insufferable, and for the first time, the chief judge Honoré Syntax had to give his youthful offspring a taste of the whip.

In the school, there was a veritable riot, and dictionaries flew across the classrooms in deplorable trajectories. The pupils could no longer be kept in order, and in any case the state of overexcitement even spread to their teachers, who piled onto them one extravagant punishment after another.

There was yet another phenomenon! All these Quiquendonians, hitherto so sober, whose nourishment consisted principally of whipped cream, started to indulge in veritable orgies of food and drink. Their usual diet was no longer sufficient. Every stomach was transformed into a chasm, and this chasm had to be filled by the most energetic means. The town's consumption tripled. Instead of two meals, they ate six. Numerous cases of indigestion were reported. Councillor Niklausse could not sate his hunger. Burgomaster van Tricasse could not assuage his thirst, and was now permanently in a sort of semi-drunken rage.

Eventually, the most alarming symptoms appeared, and spread from day to day.

You came across people who were drunk – and often they were town notables.

Stomach pains kept Dr Dominique Custos exceptionally busy, as well as cases of neuritis and neurophlogosis, which clearly proved to what degree of irritability the populace's nerves had been so strangely wrought.

There were daily quarrels and altercations in the streets of Quiquendone, formerly so deserted, and now so thronged; no one could stay at home any more.

They had to form a new police force to keep in check all those disturbers of public order.

A lock-up was installed in the town hall, and it was filled

night and day with hardened lawbreakers. Commissioner Passauf had his work cut out.

A marriage was contracted in less than two months! Such a thing had never been seen before. Yes! The son of the tax collector, Rupp, married the daughter of the beautiful Augustine de Rovere – a mere fifty-seven days after he had asked for her hand!

Other marriages were decided on, that in earlier days would have remained at the planning stage for entire years. The burgomaster couldn't get over it, and he sensed that his daughter, the charming Suzel, was slipping out of his hands.

As for dear Aunty Némance, she had made so bold as to sound out Commissioner Passauf on a union which seemed to her to combine all the ingredients of happiness: wealth, standing, youth!...

Finally – horror of horrors – a duel took place! Yes, a pistol duel, with horse pistols, at seventy-five paces, with free shots! And who fought this duel? Our readers won't believe it.

It was fought between M. Frantz Niklausse, the gentle fisherman, and the son of the opulent banker, young Simon Collaert.

And the cause of this duel was the burgomaster's own daughter, with whom Simon had fallen madly in love, and whom he was unwilling to yield to the suit of a presumptuous rival.

The duel took place near the Oudenaarde Gate. The adversaries each took up position on a bank of the Vaar, Frantz on the left, Simon on the right. This was the first time such a spectacle had been presented to the inhabitants of Quiquendone. And so a packed crowd was lining the course of the Vaar.

One hundred and twenty-seven shots were exchanged without any damage to the combatants, who bore themselves with the greatest dignity, but forty-three bystanders did pick up the odd graze or two.

Seeing this, the seconds, visibly disquieted for their own safety, finally declared that honour had been satisfied!

*In which the Quiquendonians
adopt a heroic resolution*

It is easy to see the deplorable state in which the population of Quiquendone found itself. Their minds were seething. They no longer knew or recognised each other. The most pacific of people had become quarrelsome. It was dangerous to look at them askance – they would soon have sent round their seconds to your home. Some of them let their moustaches grow, and several of them – the most pugnacious – curled them up into points.

In these conditions, municipal administration and the maintenance of order in the streets and public buildings became really difficult, as the services hadn't been organised for such a situation. The burgomaster – that worthy van Tricasse whom we have known to be so gentle, so self-effacing, so incapable of taking a single decision – the burgomaster was in a constant fury. His house echoed to the roar of his voice. He issued twenty decrees a day, was always dressing down his officials, and was ready to take charge himself of the execution of his administration's laws.

Ah! What a change! That pleasant and tranquil house in which dwelt the burgomaster, that fine Flemish dwelling-place: where now was its wonted calm? What domestic squabbles followed one another now! Mme van Tricasse had become cantankerous, crotchety – a real scold. Her husband managed perhaps to drown out the sound of her voice by shouting even louder than she did, but he couldn't get her to shut up. This worthy woman took out her constant bad temper on everyone and everything around her. Nothing worked properly! The servants were slacking. Everything was late! She accused Lotchè, and even Aunty Némance, her sister-in-law, who, just as bad-tempered, gave as good as she got. Naturally, M. van Tricasse took the side of his servant Lotchè, as happens in all households. Hence the permanent exasperation of the burgomaster's wife, and the scoldings, arguments, disputes, and rows that went on and on!

'Whatever can be wrong with us?' the unhappy burgomaster kept exclaiming. 'What is this fire consuming us? Are we possessed by the devil? Ah! Madame van Tricasse, Madame van Tricasse! You'll end up forcing me to die before you, and thereby fail to honour all the family traditions!'

The reader won't, of course, have forgotten this somewhat bizarre detail, that M. van Tricasse was supposed to become a widower and remarry, so as not to break the chain of convention.

Meanwhile this new psychological tendency produced yet other effects, rather curious ones that are worth mentioning. This overexcitement, whose cause we have yet to discover, led to types of physiological regeneration that no one could have anticipated. Talents that would have once been left fallow now set their possessors apart from the crowd. Aptitudes were revealed. Artists who until then had been quite mediocre showed themselves in a new light. Men appeared on the political as well as the literary scene. Orators learnt their skills from the most arduous debates, and on every question they fired an audience that was in any case already perfectly primed to catch fire. From council sessions, the momentum passed into public gatherings, and a political club was founded at Quiquendone, while twenty newspapers – the *Quiquendone Observer*, the *Quiquendone Independent*, the *Quiquendone Radical*, the *Quiquendone Extremist* –

all written in rage, tackled the gravest social questions.

But what did they write about? the reader will wonder. About everything and nothing; about the Oudenaarde Tower that was leaning (some wanted to knock it down and others wanted to restore it to the vertical); about the by-laws that the council was issuing, which ill-intentioned persons were trying to resist; about the sweeping of the gutters and the cleaning of the sewers, etc. And it would have been all right if the fiery orators had merely attacked the local municipal administration. No: swept away in the torrent, they had to go even further and, unless Providence intervened, to drag, push and plunge their fellows into the hazards of war.

The fact was that for eight or nine hundred years, Quiquendone had been sitting on a *casus belli* of the finest quality; but the town guarded it preciously, like a relic, and it seemed to have every chance of going stale and losing its potential usefulness.

Here is the reason that lay behind that *casus belli*.

It is not widely known that Quiquendone lies, in this fine corner of Flanders, next to the small town of Virgamen. The territories of these two free towns border with each other.

Now, in 1195, some time before the departure of Count Baldwin for the crusade, a cow from Virgamen (not, indeed – note well! – the cow of one of the inhabitants, but a communal cow) came to graze on the territory of Quiquendone. This wretched ruminant barely

Cropped thrice its tongue's breadth from the grassy mead,

but the misdemeanour, the offence, the crime, as you will, was committed and duly set down in the written record of the time – for in this period magistrates were starting to be literate.

'We will avenge ourselves when the time comes,' Natalis van Tricasse, the thirty-second predecessor of the current burgomaster, contented himself with saying, 'and the Virgamenians won't lose anything by waiting.'

The Virgamenians were warned. They waited, thinking, not without reason, that the memory of the injury would fade with time; and indeed, for several centuries, they lived on good terms with their fellows in Quiquendone.

But they hadn't reckoned with their hosts, or rather with that strange epidemic which, changing radically the character of their neighbours, awoke in those hearts the slumbering desire for vengeance.

It was in the club in the rue Monstrelet that the fiery-tempered Barrister Schut, suddenly throwing the question at his audience, aroused their passions by employing the expressions and metaphors that are usual in these circumstances. He reminded them of the offence; he reminded them of the wrong done to the free town of Quiquendone, for which a nation 'zealous to safeguard its rights' could not admit any statute of limitation; he showed them the injury still fresh, the wound still bleeding; he spoke of a certain way of shaking their heads peculiar to the inhabitants of Virgamen, indicating the contempt they felt for the inhabitants of Quiquendone; he begged his compatriots, who, 'unawares' perhaps, had put up with this mortal insult for several long centuries; he adjured 'the children of this ancient town' to have no other 'objective' but that of obtaining manifest reparation! Finally, he appealed to 'all the vital strength' of the nation!

The enthusiasm with which these words, so new to Quiquendonian ears, were received can be felt but not expressed. All the listeners had risen to their feet and, arms outstretched, called for war at the tops of their voices. Never had Barrister Schut met with such success, and it has to be admitted that he had cut a really fine figure.

The burgomaster, the councillor, all the notables present at this memorable session, would have been powerless to resist the strength of feeling among the people. In any case, they had no desire to do so, and they were shouting, if not more loudly, at least every bit as loudly as the others:

'To the frontier! To the frontier!'

Now, as the frontier was only three kilometres away from the walls of Quiquendone, it is certain that the Virgamenians were in real danger; they could be invaded before having had time to mobilise.

However, the honourable chemist, Josse Liefrinck, who alone had preserved his common sense at this grave juncture, tried to point out that they didn't have rifles, cannons, or generals.

Back came the reply – accompanied by a few punches and jostlings – that those generals, those cannons, and those rifles could be improvised; the righteousness of one's cause and the love of one's country were enough to make a people unstoppable.

Whereupon the burgomaster himself addressed the audience, and in a sublime improvised speech he did justice to those feeble-hearted characters, those who disguise fear under the veil of caution; and he tore this veil away with his patriotic hand.

You could easily have imagined, at this moment, that the hall would be brought down by the storm of applause.

A vote was requested.

The vote was passed by a unanimous show of hands, and the shouts grew even louder:

'To Virgamen! To Virgamen!'

The burgomaster then committed himself to mobilising the armies, and in the name of the whole town he promised whichever of his future generals would return victorious all the honours of a triumph, as was the custom in Roman times.

Meanwhile the chemist Josse Liefrinck, who was a stubborn fellow, and who refused to accept that he had been beaten, even though he really had been, tried to make himself heard again. He noted that in Rome a triumph was granted to victorious generals only when they had killed five thousand of the enemy's men...

'Well? So what!' exclaimed all present, beside themselves.

'...And the population of the free town of Virgamen does not exceed 3,575 inhabitants, so it will be difficult, unless you kill the same person several times over...'

But the unhappy logician was not allowed to finish, and, battered and bruised all over, he was thrown out.

'Citizens,' said Sylvestre Pulmacher, who was in ordinary life a retail grocer, 'citizens, whatever that cowardly chemist may have said, I personally promise to kill five thousand Virgamenians, if you will accept my services.'

'Five thousand, five hundred!' a more resolute patriot shouted out.

'Six thousand, six hundred!' replied the grocer.

'Seven thousand!' cried the confectioner from the rue Hemling, Jean Orbideck, who was in the process of making a fortune from the sale of whipped cream.

'Going! Going! Gone!' cried Burgomaster van Tricasse, seeing that no one was raising the bidding.

And that is how the confectioner Jean Orbideck became general-in-chief of the troops of Quiquendone.

*In which assistant Ygène utters a reasonable
remark which is forcefully rejected by Dr Ox*

'Well, master!' assistant Ygène began the following day, as he poured buckets of sulphuric acid into his huge trough-batteries.

'Well!' continued Dr Ox, 'wasn't I right? Now you can see what determines not just the physical development of a whole nation, but also its morality, its dignity, its talents, its political sense! It's merely a matter of molecules…'

'Doubtless, but…'

'But?…'

'Don't you think that things have gone far enough, and we shouldn't overexcite those poor devils too much?'

'No! no!' exclaimed the doctor, 'no! I'm going to go all the way.'

'Whatever you want, master, but the experiment seems conclusive to me, and I think it's high time to…'

'To?…'

'To close the tap.'

'You can't be serious!' exclaimed Dr Ox. 'If you dare do such a thing, I'll throttle you!'

*In which it is proved once again that from a lofty
position one can gaze down on all human pettiness*

'You were saying?' Burgomaster van Tricasse asked Councillor Niklausse.

'I was saying that this war is necessary,' replied the councillor firmly, 'and that the time has come to avenge our injury.'

'And *I*,' replied the burgomaster with asperity, '*I* will merely tell you once again that, if the populace of Quiquendone were not to take advantage of this opportunity to demand its rights, it would be unworthy of its name.'

'And *I* maintain that we must brook no delay in assembling our cohorts and leading them forward.'

'Come, come, monsieur!' replied van Tricasse, 'who do you think you're talking to?'

'To you, Burgomaster, and you will hear the truth, however hard it is for you.'

'And *you* will hear it too, Councillor!' retorted van Tricasse, beside himself. 'It will be truer coming from my lips than from yours! Yes, monsieur, yes: any delay would be dishonourable. The town of Quiquendone has been waiting for an opportunity to take its revenge for nine hundred years, and whatever you might say, whether it suits you or not, we are going to march on the enemy!'

'Aha! So that's the way you want it!' replied Councillor Niklausse vehemently. 'Well, monsieur, we will march without you if you prefer not to come with us.'

'The place of a burgomaster is at the head of his troops, monsieur.'

'And so is that of a councillor, monsieur.'

'You are insulting me by your words and trying to thwart my every wish!' cried the burgomaster, whose fists were showing a tendency to change into projectiles ready to lash out.

'And you are insulting me by casting doubts on my patriotism!' cried Niklausse; he too had struck an aggressive pose.

'Let me tell you, monsieur, that the Quiquendonian army will be marching within two days!'

'And let *me* tell *you*, monsieur, not for the first time, that we will have marched on the enemy within the next forty-eight hours!'

It is easy to observe from this fragment of conversation that the two parties in the discussion were proposing exactly the same idea. Both of them wanted to join battle, but as their overexcitement impelled them to quarrel, Niklausse wasn't listening to van Tricasse and van Tricasse wasn't listening to Niklausse. Even if they had held opposite views on this grave question, even if the burgomaster had wanted war and the councillor had held out for peace, the altercation could not have been more violent. Those two former friends glared at each other in rage. From their accelerated heartbeats, their flushed faces, their contracted pupils, their trembling muscles, and their voices, which were almost roaring, it was easy to see that they were ready to throw themselves at one another.

But the chiming of a big clock fortunately halted the adversaries just at the moment they were about to come to blows.

'At last, it's time!' cried the burgomaster.

'Time for what?' asked the councillor.

'Time to go to the belfry tower.'

'Quite right, and whether you like it or not, that's just where I'm going, monsieur.'

'Me too.'

'Let's go!'

'Let's go!'

These last words might lead one to suppose that a duel was about to take place and that the adversaries were making their way to the spot where they were to fight. But nothing could have been further from the truth. It had been agreed that the burgomaster and the councillor – in reality the two principle notables of the town – would make their way to the town hall; there, they would climb the tower, which rose to a great height above it, and examine the surrounding countryside so as to make the best strategic plans to ensure the successful advance of their troops.

Although they were both agreed on this subject, they didn't stop quarrelling all the way there, with the most deplorable acerbity. The sound of their voices raised in anger could be heard echoing through the streets, but as all the passers-by were at the same high pitch of fever, their exasperation seemed natural, and no one paid them any attention. In these circumstances, a calm man would have been considered a monster.

By the time they reached the porch of the belfry, the burgomaster and the councillor were in a paroxysm of rage. They were no longer red in the face, but pale. This terrible quarrel, despite the fact they actually agreed with one another, had shaken them to the pit of their stomachs, and as everyone knows, pallor proves that anger has reached its ultimate limits.

At the foot of the narrow belfry stairwell, there was a veritable explosion. Who would be the first to go up? Who would be the first to climb the steps of the spiral staircase?

The truth obliges us to say that there was a scuffle, and that Councillor Niklausse, forgetting everything he owed his superior, the supreme magistrate of the town, shoved van Tricasse out of the way and dashed ahead up the winding stairs.

As the two of them charged headlong up the staircase, at first taking four steps in each stride, they hurled the most objectionable epithets at one another. It was enough to make anyone afraid that things would come to a dreadful conclusion at the summit of this tower, which was 357 feet above street level.

But the two enemies soon ran out of breath, and, after a minute, by the time they reached the eightieth step, they were reduced to climbing laboriously, panting heavily.

But then – maybe it was a consequence of their breathlessness – if their anger did not abate, at least it no longer found expression in a series of indecorous terms of abuse. They were now silent and, strange to relate, it seemed that their overemotional state faded as they climbed higher over the town. Their minds became, as it were, more tranquil. The seething in their brains diminished, just as the bubbling and boiling in a coffee pot stops when you take it off the fire. Why?

To this question why, we have no answer; but the fact of the matter is that, once they had reached a certain landing, 270 feet above the level of the town, the two adversaries sat down and, looking really and truly calmer, stared at each other without anger, so to speak.

'How high it is!' said the burgomaster, wiping his handkerchief over his rubicund face.

'Very high!' replied the councillor. 'Do you know we're fourteen feet higher than the Saint Michaelis tower in Hamburg?'

'Yes, I know,' replied the burgomaster with a trace of vanity in his voice – quite forgivable in the foremost figure of authority in Quiquendone.

After a few moments, the two notables continued their upward march, glancing curiously through the loopholes pierced in the walls of the tower. The burgomaster had moved to the head of the caravan without the councillor making the slightest objection. Indeed, at around the three hundred and fourth step, as van Tricasse was absolutely shattered, Niklausse gave him a friendly push up from behind. The burgomaster made no demur and, when he arrived at the summit of the tower, said graciously:

'Thank you, Niklausse, that's one good turn I owe you.'

Not long before, when they had arrived at the foot of the tower, they had been two wild beasts ready to tear each other apart; now, as they reached its summit, they were two friends.

The weather was magnificent. It was May. The sun had burned away all the haze. What a pure and limpid atmosphere! The smallest objects could be seen within a considerable radius. Only a few miles away you could make out the walls of Virgamen, dazzlingly white, its red roofs pointing up here and there, and its spires dappled with sunlight. And this was the town foredoomed to all the horrors of pillage and fire!

The burgomaster and the councillor had sat next to each other on a little stone bench, like two fine fellows whose souls merge and mingle in a close harmony. While getting their breath back, they gazed out; then, after a few moments of silence, the burgomaster exclaimed:

'How beautiful it is!'

'Yes, it's wonderful!' replied the councillor. 'Doesn't it seem to you, my worthy van Tricasse, that humanity is destined rather to remain at these heights than to creep and crawl about on the crust of our round earth?'

'I agree with you, honest Niklausse,' replied the burgomaster, 'I agree with you. It is easier to sense the emotions that emanate from nature! You can breathe them in through all your senses! It's at these altitudes that philosophers should learn their trade, and it's here that wise men should live, far above the miseries of this world!'

'Shall we walk round the platform?' asked the councillor.

'Let's walk round the platform,' replied the burgomaster.

And the two friends, leaning on one another's arms, and leaving, as had been their wont, long pauses between their questions and their answers, examined every point of the horizon.

'It's been at least seventeen years since I came up on the belfry tower,' said van Tricasse.

'I don't think I've ever been up,' replied councillor Niklausse, 'and I regret it; from this height the view is sublime! Can you see, my dear friend, the pretty river Vaar down there, winding between the trees?'

'And further on, the heights of Sainte-Hermandad! How gracefully they ring the horizon round! Look at that row of green trees that Nature has arranged in such a picturesque fashion! Ah! Nature, Nature, Niklausse! Could the hand of man ever rival her?'

'It's enchanting, my excellent friend,' replied the councillor. 'Look at those herds chewing the cud in the verdant meadows, those oxen, those cows, those sheep...'

'And the labourers going out to work in the fields! They look like shepherds from Arcadia. All they need is a little bagpipe!'

'And stretching out over all this fertile countryside, the lovely blue sky, untroubled by a single cloud! Ah, Niklausse, one could become a poet here! My word, I don't understand why St Simeon Stylites wasn't one of the greatest poets in the world.'[9]

'It's perhaps because his column wasn't high enough!' replied the councillor, with a gentle smile.

At this moment, the Quiquendone chimes started to peal. The limpid bells played one of their most melodious tunes. The two friends were thrown into raptures at the sound.

Then, in his calm voice, the burgomaster said:

'But, friend Niklausse, why are we here at the summit of this tower?'

'Well,' replied the councillor, 'we're letting ourselves get carried away by daydreams…'

'Why are we here?' repeated the burgomaster.

'We are here,' replied Niklausse, 'to breathe this pure air that has not been sullied by human weakness.'

'Well then, shall we go down, friend Niklausse?'

'Let's go down, friend van Tricasse.'

The two notables glanced one last time at the splendid panorama spread out before their eyes; then the burgomaster went ahead, and began to go down with a slow, measured pace. The councillor followed him, a few steps behind him. The two notables reached the landing where they had rested on the way up. Already their cheeks were starting to get flushed. They stopped for a moment and then resumed their interrupted descent.

After a minute, van Tricasse requested Niklausse to moderate his pace, since he could feel him hot on his heels and 'it irritated him'.

It did more than just irritate him: twenty steps lower, he ordered the councillor to stand still, so he could get a bit of a head start on him.

The councillor replied that he didn't feel like standing there with one leg in the air, waiting on the good pleasure of the burgomaster, and he continued.

Van Tricasse replied with a somewhat harsh expression.

The councillor retorted with a wounding allusion to the advanced age of the burgomaster, destined as he was, by his family traditions, to marry for a second time.

The burgomaster descended another twenty steps, informing Niklausse in no uncertain terms that it wasn't going to be like that.

Niklausse replied that, anyway, *he* was going to go down first; and as the stairwell was very narrow, there was a collision between the two notables, who were just then in deepest darkness.

The words 'great oaf' and 'clumsy idiot' were the mildest of the insults that were then exchanged.

'We'll see, you stupid fool,' cried the burgomaster, 'we'll see what kind of a figure you cut in this war, and in which rank you march!'

'In the rank ahead of yours, you silly idiot!' replied Niklausse.

Then they exchanged other cries of abuse, and it was as if their two bodies were rolling together...

What happened? Why did their moods change so rapidly? Why did the sheep on the tower platform become transformed into tigers, two hundred feet lower down?

Whatever the answer, the tower warden, hearing such a racket, came to open the lower door right at the moment the two adversaries, battered and bruised, their eyes popping out of their heads, were pulling each other's hair out (fortunately, they both wore wigs).

'You will give me satisfaction!' shouted the burgomaster, waving his fist under his adversary's nose.

'Whenever you like!' bellowed Councillor Niklausse, drawing back his right foot and leaving it hovering there menacingly.

The warden, who was himself in a furious temper – nobody knows why – found this scene of mutual provocation perfectly natural. I don't know what personal overexcitement was tempting him to join in the fray. But he restrained himself and went to spread, throughout the entire district, the news that a duel was shortly to take place between Burgomaster van Tricasse and Councillor Niklausse.

*In which things are taken so far that the inhabitants
of Quiquendone, the readers, and even the author
demand that it all be brought to an end*

This final incident proves how high the level of emotional intensity in the Quiquendonian populace had risen. For the two most long-standing friends in the town, and the most mild-mannered – before the invasion of the malady – to reach this degree of violence! And for this to happen only a few minutes after their former mutual liking, their friendly instincts, their contemplative temperaments, had started to gain the upper hand at the summit of the tower!

When he learnt what was happening, Dr Ox could not contain his joy. He resisted the arguments of his assistant, in whose view things were taking a turn for the worse. In any case, both of them were every bit as overexcited as the rest of the population, and they ended up quarrelling just as much as the burgomaster and the councillor.

Furthermore, it must be said, one question was dominating all the others, and had obliged them to put off their planned duel until the Virgamenian question had been settled. No one had the right to shed his blood uselessly when every last drop of it belonged to the beleaguered fatherland.

It was true: circumstances were grave, and there was no going back.

Burgomaster van Tricasse, for all the warlike ardour with which he was impelled, had not felt he could throw himself on his enemy without first warning him. So he had, through the intermediary of the country policeman, M. Hotteringe, called upon the Virgamenians to make reparation for the injustice committed in 1195 on the territory of Quiquendone.

The authorities of Virgamen had at first been unable to guess what it was all about, and the country policeman, despite his official status, had been shown the door in a very cavalier fashion.

Then van Tricasse sent one of the aides-de-camp of the confectioner and general, Citizen Hildevert Shuman, a barley-sugar manufacturer, a man of great firmness and forcefulness, who conveyed to the authorities of Virgamen the very record of the proceedings drawn up in 1195 by Burgomaster Natalis van Tricasse.

The authorities of Virgamen burst out laughing, and the aide-de-camp met with exactly the same fate as the country policeman.

Then the burgomaster assembled the town notables. A letter, composed in remarkable, vigorous terms, was issued as an ultimatum; the *casus belli* was clearly indicated, and a time limit of twenty-four hours was set for the guilty town to make reparation for the outrage done to Quiquendone.

The letter went off, and came back, a few hours later, torn into tiny pieces, which constituted so many new insults. The Virgamenians had long known of the forbearance of the Quiquendonians, and they couldn't care less about them, their demands, their *casus belli*, or their ultimatum.

There was only one thing left to do: resort to arms, call on the god of battles and, following the Prussian method, throw themselves on the Virgamenians before they were altogether ready.

This was the decision reached by the council in a solemn session, in which shouts, admonitions, and threatening gestures were exchanged with unprecedented violence. A gathering of lunatics, a club of men possessed by devils could not have been any more tumultuous.

As soon as the declaration of war had been made public, General Jean Orbideck assembled his troops, more than two thousand combatants out of a population of 2,393 souls. Women, children and old men had all joined the adult men. Any object that could be used to cut or hit had become a weapon. The town's rifles had been requisitioned. Five of them had been discovered, two of them without hammers, and they had been distributed to the vanguard. The artillery comprised the old culverin of the castle, captured in 1339 during the attack on le Quesnoy – one of the first pieces of ordnance mentioned in history; it hadn't been fired for five centuries. In any case, there wasn't any projectile to load it with, fortunately for those manning it, but, as it was, this war machine could still strike fear into the enemy. As for the weapons of hand-to-hand combat, they had been gathered from the museum of antiquities: flint axes, helms, maces, Frankish battleaxes and javelins, gisarmes, partisans, verderers, rapiers, etc., and also from those individual arsenals generally known as *pantries* and *kitchens*. But courage, justice, hatred of the foreigner, and the desire for vengeance would have to stand in for more elaborate weapons and replace – or so they at least hoped – modern machine guns and breech-loading cannons.

An inspection was held. Not a single citizen failed to appear at the roll-call. General Orbideck, a little unsteady on his horse – a wily beast – fell off, three times, in front of the army, but he got up again uninjured, which was taken as a favourable omen. The burgomaster, the councillor, the civil commissioner, the great judge, the tax collector, the banker, the rector, in short all the notables of the town walked at the head. There was not a single tear shed by their mothers, or their sisters, or their daughters. They pushed their husbands, their fathers, and their brothers on into combat, and even followed on behind, forming a rearguard under the command of the courageous Mme van Tricasse.

The trumpet of the town crier Jean Mistrol rang out; the army stepped forward, left the square and, uttering fierce cries, headed off towards the Oudenaarde Gate.

Just as the head of the column was about to cross the walls of the town, a man threw himself in front of it.

'Stop! Stop! You fools!' he cried. 'Don't start fighting! Let me close the tap! You are not athirst for blood! You are nice, mild-tempered, peaceable folk! If you are so inflamed, it's all the fault of my master, Dr Ox! It's an experiment! He claimed to be providing you with lighting fuelled by oxyhydric gas, but it was a pretext to saturate…'

The assistant was beside himself, but he couldn't finish. Just as the doctor's secret was about to escape from his lips, Dr Ox himself, in an indescribable fury, hurled himself on the unfortunate Ygène, and reduced him to silence with a punch on the mouth.

All hell was let loose. The burgomaster, the councillor and the notables, who had halted at the sight of Ygène, were in turn swept away by their exasperation, and flung themselves onto the two strangers, refusing to hear either of them speak. Dr Ox and his assistant, jostled and beaten, were just about to be dragged off to the lock-up, on the orders of van Tricasse, when…

In which the story ends with a bang

…When a huge explosion rocked the air. The whole atmosphere in which Quiquendone was wrapped seemed to have been set on fire. A flame of phenomenal intensity and brightness shot up like a meteor high into the sky. If it had been night time, its blaze would have been visible for a radius of ten leagues.

The whole army of Quiquendone was lying flat on its faces, like an army of capuchin monks… Fortunately, there were no casualties: a few grazes and a few bumps and bruises, that was all. The confectioner, who by pure chance hadn't fallen off his horse this time, got the plume of his helmet singed, and escaped without any other injury.

What had happened?

Quite simply, as they soon learnt, the gas factory had exploded. During the absence of the doctor and his assistant, someone had probably done something careless. Nobody knows how or why the reservoir containing oxygen and the reservoir containing hydrogen had been linked together. From the mixing of these two gases, an explosive mixture had resulted, to which a light was accidentally set.

This changed everything; – but when the army picked itself up, Dr Ox and the assistant Ygène had disappeared.

16

*In which the intelligent reader clearly sees that he had
guessed correctly, despite all the author's precautions*

After the explosion, Quiquendone had immediately turned
back into the peaceful, phlegmatic and Flemish town that it had
been before.

After the explosion – which didn't actually cause that
much of a stir – everyone, without knowing why, mechanically
took himself off home, the burgomaster leaning on the arm
of the councillor, Barrister Schut on the arm of Dr Custos,
Frantz Niklausse on the arm of his rival Simon Collaert, each of
them tranquilly and quietly, without even being aware of what
had happened, having already forgotten Virgamen and vengeance. The general had gone back to making confectionery,
and his aide-de-camp to his barley-sugar.

Calm had been restored throughout the town, and
everything had reverted to its habitual way of life: men and
animals, animals and plants, even the Oudenaarde Tower,
which the explosion – these explosions can be so surprising –
had restored to the vertical!

And ever since then, not one word raised in anger, not
a single argument in the town of Quiquendone. No more
politics, no more clubs, no more lawsuits, no more policemen!
The job of Commissioner Passauf was soon once more a
sinecure, and if his salary wasn't taken away from him, it
was because the burgomaster and the councillor couldn't
make up their minds to make up their minds about him.
In any case, from time to time, he continued to glide, without
even realising it, through the dreams of the inconsolable Aunty
Némance.

As for Frantz's rival, he nobly abandoned the charming Suzel to her lover, who married her in haste, five or six years after these events.

And as for Mme van Tricasse, she died ten years later, meeting her deadline as expected, and the burgomaster married Mlle Pélagie van Tricasse, her charming cousin, in fortunate circumstances... for the happy mortal who was to succeed him.

17

In which Dr Ox's theory is explained

So what had this mysterious Dr Ox done? Carried out a whimsical experiment, that was all. After having set up his gas pipes, he had saturated the public monuments, then the private houses, and finally the streets of Quiquendone with pure oxygen, without a single atom of hydrogen to keep it company.

Oxygen, tasteless and odourless, diffused at such a high dose through the atmosphere, causes, when inhaled, the most serious disturbances to the organism. When you live in an environment saturated by oxygen you become excited, over-excited – inflamed! Once you have returned to an ordinary atmosphere, you turn back into your normal self; this was the case for the councillor and the burgomaster, when, at the top of the belfry tower, they found themselves breathing normal fresh air again, as the oxygen, being heavier, remained confined to the lower levels.

But also, if you live in conditions like these, and breathe this gas which physiologically transforms the body as well as the soul, you soon die, like those madmen who lead lives of extravagant intensity!

It was thus fortunate for the Quiquendonians that a providential explosion intervened to bring this dangerous experiment to an end, by destroying Dr Ox's factory.

In short, and in conclusion, might it be that virtue, courage, talent, intelligence and imagination – all these qualities or faculties – are nothing but a question of oxygen?

Such is the theory of Dr Ox, but we have every right not to accept it, despite his whimsical experiment, for which the honourable town of Quiquendone provided the setting.

NOTES

1. Adolphe Joanne (1813–81) was a French geographer and author of numerous guidebooks.

2. A reference to the creation of the Kingdom of Belgium in 1831.

3. Jeannot was, in French fable, the man who replaced alternately the worn-out blades and handles of his knife, while still considering it to be the same knife.

4. Harpocrates was the Greek name for the Egyptian god Horus, regarded by the Romans as the god of silence.

5. Preterition and aposiopesis are figures of rhetoric in which, respectively, a thing is referred to by professing to omit it, or there is a sudden breaking-off in speech.

6. *In anima vili* is a Latin term referring to an experiment performed on an expendable subject.

7. Hervé (the professional name of Florimond Ronger, 1825–92) was a composer of comic operas, including *L'Oeil crevé* (1867). Jacques Offenbach (1819–80) was also a composer, best known for the opera *La Belle Hélène* (1864).

8. *Robert le Diable* (1831) and *Les Huguenots* (1836) are two famous operas by Giacomo Meyerbeer (1791–1864); *William Tell* (1829) is a work by Gioacchino Rossini (1792–1868).

9. St Simeon Stylites spent much of his life atop a series of pillars in the desert.

BIOGRAPHICAL NOTE

Jules Gabriel Verne was born in 1828 in Nantes, France. His father, Pierre, was a lawyer, and his mother, Sophie Allotte, came from a family of ship builders and sea captains. Verne's father intended that he should become a lawyer, but Verne refused to do anything but write. In 1848 he went to Paris, supposedly to study law, but in fact to further his literary career. There he met with Victor Hugo and Alexandre Dumas, who encouraged him to write historical novels, a popular literary genre at that time. Verne disliked the historical novel, however, and set about writing articles, short stories and plays instead, one of which, *The Broken Straws*, was performed in 1850. That same year, Verne's father learnt that his son had abandoned his studies and so discontinued his allowance; Verne was therefore forced to sell stories for a living.

After continuing to write for years with little success, in 1863 Verne wrote *Five Weeks in a Balloon*, the first of a successful cycle of sixty-three novels of adventure and fantasy. Initially refused for publication because it was considered too scientific and not sufficiently exciting or adventurous, it was finally published by a press that specialised in children's books. It was translated into many languages and Verne found that he had become both rich and famous.

Verne took an active interest in the latest scientific knowledge and current theories about the earth, and his works – *Journey to the Centre of the Earth* (1864), *From the Earth to the Moon* (1865), *20,000 Leagues Under the Sea* (1870) and *Around the World in Eighty Days* (1873) among them – reflected this passion, and have earned Verne the title of the founder of modern science fiction.

Verne died on 24th March 1905 in the city of Amiens.

Andrew Brown studied at the University of Cambridge, where he taught French for many years. He now works as a freelance teacher and translator. He is the author of *Roland Barthes: the Figures of Writing* (OUP, 1993), and his translations include *Memoirs of a Madman* by Gustave Flaubert, *For a Night of Love* by Emile Zola, *The Jinx* by Théophile Gautier, *Mademoiselle de Scudéri* by E.T.A. Hoffmann, *Theseus* by André Gide, *Incest* by Marquis de Sade, *The Ghost-seer* by Friedrich von Schiller, *Colonel Chabert* by Honoré de Balzac, *Memoirs of an Egotist* by Stendhal, *Butterball* by Guy de Maupassant, and *With the Flow* by Joris-Karl Huysmans, all published by Hesperus Press.

HESPERUS PRESS – 100 PAGES

Hesperus Press, as suggested by the Latin motto, is committed to bringing near what is far – far both in space and time. Works written by the greatest authors, and unjustly neglected or simply little known in the English-speaking world, are made accessible through new translations and a completely fresh editorial approach. Through these short classic works, each around 100 pages in length, the reader will be introduced to the greatest writers from all times and all cultures.

For more information on Hesperus Press, please visit our website: **www.hesperuspress.com**

ET REMOTISSIMA PROPE

SELECTED TITLES FROM HESPERUS PRESS

Author	Title	Foreword writer
Pietro Aretino	*The School of Whoredom*	Paul Bailey
Jane Austen	*Love and Friendship*	Fay Weldon
Honoré de Balzac	*Colonel Chabert*	A.N. Wilson
Charles Baudelaire	*On Wine and Hashish*	Margaret Drabble
Giovanni Boccaccio	*Life of Dante*	A.N. Wilson
Charlotte Brontë	*The Green Dwarf*	Libby Purves
Mikhail Bulgakov	*The Fatal Eggs*	Doris Lessing
Giacomo Casanova	*The Duel*	Tim Parks
Miguel de Cervantes	*The Dialogue of the Dogs*	
Anton Chekhov	*The Story of a Nobody*	Louis de Bernières
Wilkie Collins	*Who Killed Zebedee?*	Martin Jarvis
Arthur Conan Doyle	*The Tragedy of the Korosko*	Tony Robinson
William Congreve	*Incognita*	Peter Ackroyd
Joseph Conrad	*Heart of Darkness*	A.N. Wilson
Gabriele D'Annunzio	*The Book of the Virgins*	Tim Parks
Dante Alighieri	*New Life*	Louis de Bernières
Daniel Defoe	*The King of Pirates*	Peter Ackroyd
Marquis de Sade	*Incest*	Janet Street-Porter
Charles Dickens	*The Haunted House*	Peter Ackroyd
Fyodor Dostoevsky	*Poor People*	Charlotte Hobson
Joseph von Eichendorff	*Life of a Good-for-nothing*	
George Eliot	*Amos Barton*	Matthew Sweet
F. Scott Fitzgerald	*The Rich Boy*	John Updike
Gustave Flaubert	*Memoirs of a Madman*	Germaine Greer
E.M. Forster	*Arctic Summer*	Anita Desai
Ugo Foscolo	*Last Letters of Jacopo Ortis*	Valerio Massimo Manfredi
Elizabeth Gaskell	*Lois the Witch*	Jenny Uglow

Théophile Gautier	*The Jinx*	Gilbert Adair
André Gide	*Theseus*	
Nikolai Gogol	*The Squabble*	Patrick McCabe
Thomas Hardy	*Fellow-Townsmen*	Emma Tennant
Nathaniel Hawthorne	*Rappaccini's Daughter*	Simon Schama
E.T.A. Hoffmann	*Mademoiselle de Scudéri*	Gilbert Adair
Victor Hugo	*The Last Day of a Condemned Man*	Libby Purves
Joris-Karl Huysmans	*With the Flow*	Simon Callow
Henry James	*In the Cage*	Libby Purves
Franz Kafka	*Metamorphosis*	Martin Jarvis
Heinrich von Kleist	*The Marquise of O–*	Andrew Miller
D.H. Lawrence	*The Fox*	Doris Lessing
Leonardo da Vinci	*Prophecies*	Eraldo Affinati
Giacomo Leopardi	*Thoughts*	Edoardo Albinati
Nikolai Leskov	*Lady Macbeth of Mtsensk*	Gilbert Adair
Niccolò Machiavelli	*Life of Castruccio Castracani*	Richard Overy
Katherine Mansfield	*In a German Pension*	Linda Grant
Guy de Maupassant	*Butterball*	Germaine Greer
Herman Melville	*The Enchanted Isles*	Margaret Drabble
Francis Petrarch	*My Secret Book*	Germaine Greer
Luigi Pirandello	*Loveless Love*	
Edgar Allan Poe	*Eureka*	Sir Patrick Moore
Alexander Pope	*Scriblerus*	Peter Ackroyd
Alexander Pushkin	*Dubrovsky*	Patrick Neate
François Rabelais	*Gargantua*	Paul Bailey
François Rabelais	*Pantagruel*	Paul Bailey
Friedrich von Schiller	*The Ghost-seer*	Martin Jarvis
Percy Bysshe Shelley	*Zastrozzi*	Germaine Greer
Stendhal	*Memoirs of an Egotist*	Doris Lessing
Robert Louis Stevenson	*Dr Jekyll and Mr Hyde*	Helen Dunmore